THE

Young

AND THE

Ruthless

ALSO BY VICTORIA ROWELL

The Women Who Raised Me: A Memoir
Secrets of a Soap Opera Diva
Tag, Toss & Run: 40 Classic Lawn Games

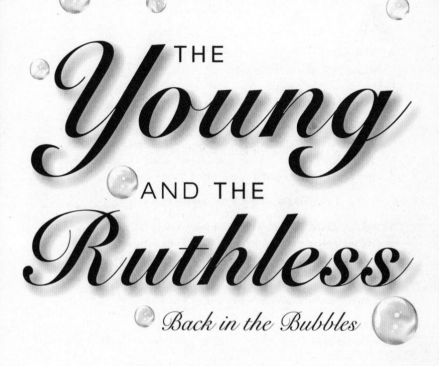

THE
Young
AND THE
Ruthless
Back in the Bubbles

VICTORIA ROWELL

ATRIA PAPERBACK

New York London Toronto Sydney New Delhi

ATRIA PAPERBACK

A Division of Simon & Schuster, Inc.
1230 Avenue of the Americas
New York, NY 10020

First Atria Paperback edition March 2013

ATRIA PAPERBACK and colophon are trademarks of Simon & Schuster, Inc.

For information about special discounts for bulk purchases, please contact Simon & Schuster Special Sales at 1-866-506-1949 or business@simonandschuster.com.

The Simon & Schuster Speakers Bureau can bring authors to your live event. For more information or to book an event contact the Simon & Schuster Speakers Bureau at 1-866-248-3049 or visit our website at www.simonspeakers.com.

Manufactured in the United States of America

10 9 8 7 6 5 4 3 2 1

Library of Congress Cataloging-in-Publication Data is available upon request.

ISBN 978-1-4516-4383-1
ISBN 978-1-4516-4384-8 (ebook)

Special Thanks

To all who support diversity and good art.
&
To Heather Lashaway, a writing partner and friend,
for bringing your indefatigable commitment,
patience, and humor to this book.
Thanks for making writing so much fun!

Champagne for your real friends, real pain for your sham friends . . . and cheers to you if you can tell the difference.

—CALYSTA JEFFRIES

THE

Young

AND THE

Ruthless

DAYTIME DRAMA DESPERATELY SEEKING DEMO-GRAPHIC? Look! Up in the air! It's a bird . . . it's a plane . . . it's . . . a soap star on a trapeze?! That's right, kids, a few of your favorite soap stars are swapping their feathers and Spanx for sequins and . . . well, tighter Spanx, sacrificing themselves on the altar of ratings to participate on the hit WBC reality show *Circus of the Soap Opera Stars*. Course, for some—say, fan favorite Calysta Jeffries, recently re-stored to her rightful role of iconic Ruby Stargazer—the circus may be a relief after life on *The Rich and the Ruthless* set. After all, tightropes have nets and tigers just bite heads off instead of stealing storylines and men! A little birdie also told me notorious party animal Toby Gorman never made it to air after crashing into a tree light in the wings while exiting the stage during dress rehearsal, busting his nose, receiving five stitches over his left eye. Bummer!

So tune in, kiddies, to the greatest show on earth at 8/7 Central, to see more egos stuffed under a big top than clowns in a car.

The Diva

CHAPTER 1

Circus of the Soap Opera Stars

*W*heeeeeeeeeeeeeeee!" Emmy Abernathy, my co-star on the number one sudser *The Rich and the Ruthless* (Gina Chiccetelli), swung upside down overhead as I prepared to climb the ladder to the tiny trapeze platform above. Clad in a revealing gold glitter bikini and tutu ensemble, Emmy forced her legs into a split.

Nervous jitters tickled my tummy as noisy chatter from the audience filtered in and Karl L. King's "Hosts of Freedom" blasted. I glanced around the madcap circus ring set full of bustling stagehands and other besequined bubblers who'd had the dubious distinction of being chosen to participate in the WBC's prime-time reality hit *Circus of the Soap Opera Stars*. Dress rehearsal had not gone well.

"Disgusting," my powder-puffed costar Phillip McQueen (Barrett Fink) had slurred due to a mild tranq paramedics fed him earlier. Firefighters rescued a hysterical Phillip, who had a fear of heights, from the trapeze bar where he'd dangled like a helpless infant. Swathed in a hideous rainbow-sequined unitard, nervously rubbing more rosin on his palms, the divo whined, "This whole fiasco has ruined my hands. They're callused, cracking, and . . ."

A stagehand interrupted. "Climb, McQueen."

I watched his unsteady progress until he made it to the staging platform, then followed. Had to admit it was exciting—the lights, music, and growing crowd adding to the energy. As the spotlight hit me, I naturally broke into a wide, crimson-lipped smile, outstretching my gloved arms like a natural showgirl. A true soap diva always steps up to the performance plate.

* * *

For my first public appearance since rejoining the soap, *The Rich and the Ruthless*'s interim executive producer, Veronica Barringer, had chosen me to be the featured star of the main trapeze act to help represent the show, overriding objections by the World Broadcast Company network, *R&R* executives, and certain viperous costars. While they'd been forced to don a civil façade since my return, blistering hatred and jealousy thrummed underneath.

I kept it movin' and did the silly preshow interviews *Cliffhanger Weekly* conducted during dress rehearsal.

"I'm so excited to be on top of an elephant! They're so wise and never forget," my *R&R* costar and friend Shannen Lassiter (Dr. Justine Lashaway) gushed to reporter Mitch Morelli. Shannen looked radiant in the red, white, and blue striped bodysuit she'd been poured into.

"So I've heard. But, Shannen, why don't we talk about what an opportunity this is for you to be seen on prime time? Many readers have asked why you haven't made the leap to prime time or film—Broadway even. You're so . . ."

". . . sexy. I already know. And that's why. My job is to be a soap opera siren and as stimulating as possible, the fans count on it. But I've got to be honest, Mitch—being too beautiful can be a real handicap. I can't tell you how many times casting directors have called my agent to say I nailed the audition but I was distractingly beautiful; if only they'd measure me by my work. I can't help it if I'm hot without trying. I know it's intimidating, but it's a gift."

"You're so right, *amada mía*," said fiery Latin costar and Shannen's current offscreen lover, Javier Vásquez (Pepe), interrupting. Picked to get in the cage with the tigers—after Emmy was almost mauled, neglecting to report she was being visited by Aunt Flo—Javier wore only a leopard-print loincloth draped around his hips, every sculpted bronze muscle glistening with baby oil.

Mitch left Shannen and Javier doing some mauling of their own as Emmy darted in to grab a piece of the press.

"Hey, Mitch, like my tutu?" she said suggestively.

"It's very gold."

"Yeah, awesome, right? Back at my fighting weight and so ready to get up on that high wire and show the world what trapezing is all about, I could just wet myself. Did the baby food diet to prepare—lost ten pounds! What's the problem, fatties? Even got a side gig pole-dancing at Club Goodhurt as part of my training; my body's my temple and it's never been bendier."

"Pole-dancing? That's an . . . interesting way to get in . . ."

"Don't, Mitch, I hear the innuendo in your voice. Nothing skeevy about it, it's incredibly artistic. I mean, I learned how to do the Caterpillar, the Bow and Arrow, the Brass Monkey . . . it was all so empowering. Who knows, I might be the next Dita Von Teese."

"Sounds like it."

Circus handler Blaze rushed over. "Emmy, darling, we're going to have to ax the high-wire act."

"What the hell?"

"I got Phillip back on board with the trapeze since he doesn't have to let go of the bar, but he's not gonna make it across that wire."

"Are you kidding me? Big friggin' baby . . . why can't Toby do it?"

Notorious soap hottie Toby Gorman had recently returned to *The Rich and the Ruthless* as my on-screen daughter Jade's amnesiac boyfriend, Axel.

Blaze bit his lip. "Toby had an . . . accident, stagehand just escorted him to the hospital for stitches. Anyway, the act is cut."

"No way! Why can't I do it solo on roller skates like we first talked about? Lisa Rinna did it back in the day."

"I don't think so. . . ."

"Calysta, honey, you're working it," said Mitch, cozying up, leaving Emmy and Blaze to their argument.

"Feel like a disco ball exploded on me," I smirked, smoothing a manicured hand down the curve of my hip.

"How's it feel to be a part of the circus?"

"Familiar. Just swappin' one set of clowns for another."

"What's it like being back on a show you had such a public falling-out with?"

"See, that's why I dig you, Mitch, you dive right on in." I laughed. "Feels good to be back home. I've always been about the work. That hasn't changed. With Augustus on the mend and Veronica behind the wheel, this show's headin' in the right direction."

"Nicely put. Anyone sour about your return?"

Playing nice for Veronica, I said, "Why don't you ask them?" indicating my costars on the set.

* * *

As Phillip swung out on his trapeze, eyes wide with fear, I peeled off one glove and tossed it, then the other, to the crowd's roaring delight.

As I leapt from the safety of the platform, legs straight, toes perfectly pointed, arching my slender back, creating a perfect silhouette, I reached out to grab Phillip's sticky, cracked hands and clung for dear life. My stomach free-falling, I swung down across the deep chasm, momentarily transported back to my childhood—a recurring dream of winging weightlessly on cables against the backdrop of an operatic prima donna—but Phillip's loosening grip slammed me back to reality.

The crowd was a blur as I streaked by, Emmy's calculating face coming into focus as I let go of Phillip's wrists and reached for hers.

Our hands linked wrist to wrist perfectly, Emmy's slicked with baby oil.

Though it must have been mere seconds, I plummeted for what felt like forever. My back hit the net, giving me an instant rope burn, launching me briefly back into the air. Above, Emmy had come up to a sitting position on the swing, her laughter obvious though unheard by the gasping crowd.

Remembering the protocol if I were to fall, I reached to give a thumbs-up to show I was okay.

An avalanche of applause erupted.

As I bounced gently in the net, I couldn't help but think the whole thing—from the damn blinding lights to the soaring up, up, up and falling down, down, down—was a perfect metaphor for my life as a soap opera star.

HOLD ON TO YOUR CHAPEAUS, DARLINGS. Your diva has just received pearl-clutching news that Shelly Montenegro, the—and how do I say this—*mature* former star of WBC's *The Daring and the Damned*, is doing a spread for *Playboy*! Said the bona fide cougar, "Can't wait! I look mah-velous and never had any work done." Well, we can't argue with that. Seems Montenegro was a favorite of party boy Heff a million years ago. Guess an underappreciated soap legend's gotta do what she's gotta do, especially after walking off the *D&D* set last month following a contract dispute. . . .

The Diva

CHAPTER 2

Every Rose
Has Its Thorns

While the reception on my return to *The Rich and the Ruthless* had been chilly, I'd managed to avoid frostbite thanks to my new ally, Veronica Barringer. Taking over for her father, my mentor, Augustus Barringer Sr., Veronica had proven to be an invaluable asset to Barringer Dramatic Series, ambitiously taking the reins, reminiscent of Augustus's style. Thanks to her, I was also a story consultant, the same title former head writer Felicia Silverstein had been demoted to. For a rich chick, Veronica was one cool lady.

"Knock-knock," said a familiar voice through the door.

"Come in."

"Hey, Calysta." Production assistant Ben Singh smiled. "You were amazing on *Circus of the Soap Opera Stars* last week."

"Thank you."

"I'd never watch that cheesy show but . . . I kinda had to. What a drag Phillip wiped out with Emmy."

"I'm sure only their egos were bruised. What brings you by?"

"Oh, I was told to check on you."

"Check on me?"

"Yeah." He fidgeted. "You know, make sure you have everything you need."

"Such as?" I asked, enjoying every second of this.

"Well, for instance, would you like your dressing room painted, new furniture, new anything?"

Appraisingly, I responded, "Hoped that woulda been handled sooner but afterthoughts have their value."

Ben's giant eyes darted.

"I'll take the show up on a fresh coat of paint and a new rug. Clearly, someone had their pet in here without the litter box."

"I don't think it was a pet," Ben said, moving the coffee table into the hallway. Rolling up the area floor covering, he mumbled, "Better get this filth out of here before you catch something."

Shannen burst through the door. "Hey, diva, we finally have a scene together! Where do you want to run lines? Oh, Ben, I didn't see you down there."

"What's new?" he groaned.

"Ben's being a sweetheart, takin' this rank rug outta here." I said.

"O-M-G, there's so much DNA on that sisal. Couldn't pay me to come in here without a Hazmat suit on," said Shannen.

With the rug over one shoulder, Ben confirmed, "I'll get the painters in here right away, Calysta. Jamaica pink, right?"

"You remembered."

"You're the only actor we've had to get custom hypoallergenic paint for."

"I'm impressed, Calysta. Not even Joan Collins got that star treatment when she did a cameo last year," Shannen reminisced.

"It's just paint. Don't give 'em that much credit," I remarked.

Bursting at the seams to fill me in on the latest soap dish, Shannen gushed, "Guess it's not a secret anymore that Veronica called a company meeting before you returned; all cast members were mandated to attend."

"Did she?"

"She laid it out."

"Laid what out?" I encouraged.

"She warned if anyone harassed you they'd be kissing a

pink slip. The kicker was she kept her focus on Emmy and Phillip. It was awesome watching them twitch."

"Wow, I knew Veronica was in my corner but . . ."

"That's not all. She said toward the end of the season several contracts would be ending due to the industry shrinking."

"Sounds ominous."

"Everyone's nervous and boosting their brownnosing so be on Hershey alert. This is going to be quite the year." Shannen mischievously giggled. Forgetting her earlier rant, she threw herself on the couch. "I'm sooo glad you're back, Calysta."

"Awww . . ."

"I mean it. It's been hell doing this dumb show without you. Like there's been a hole in *R&R* and everyone knows it—even the haters."

"Truthfully, Shannen, I've missed the show and you just as much."

"Hey, I'll bet you a trip to Jamaica that Emmy won't pass the Veronica test."

"You're on, but we both know that heifer'll fail."

Falling out with laughter, we were interrupted by the stage manager's voice over the intercom. "That's a half hour, folks. Shannen and Calysta, you're up after lunch. Scenes twenty-four, twenty-five, and twenty-six. Be camera ready."

Sucking her teeth, Shannen said, "Can you believe production is down to *one take*?"

"Veronica's takin' the EP thing seriously, don't blame her. She ain't lettin' outsiders get their sticky flypaper hands on her family's soaps any more than she has to."

"Did you hear she threw Auggie a sibling peace offering after their falling-out went public? He's listed in the *R&R* credits as a creative consultant, but he's not supposed to come on set."

The *Cliffhanger Weekly* and *Soap Suds Digest* cover story at every supermarket checkout was how *The Daring and the Damned* had torpedoed to dead last in the ratings and been on cancellation watch until the WBC offered to save it from the soap opera graveyard like so many others. After the bloodbath was over, a reluctant Augustus Barringer had given up 51 percent of his number two soap plus all of foreign distribution.

No wonder Veronica ran *R&R* with an iron fist and slept with one eye open.

"Anyway, Veronica keeps the first thing actors spit out on camera no matter what. Drives Julius absolutely bonkers. Think he was directing before you left. Max is totally chill about it though."

"Max?"

"You haven't met him yet. He's the new assistant director. Yummy with a capital YUM. If I weren't with Javier, I would totally be inappropriate with him."

"Look, Shannen," I said, standing up and stretching. "I'm dizzy with all this catch-up and I'ma faint if I don't eat. Whaddaya say we get some grub?"

Hooking arms, we headed out.

* * *

Shannen and I shot our scenes in record time, literally ushered off set by stagehands swapping out walls. Before I could take a quick breather, a noxious voice stopped me in the hall.

Serial misogynist and co-executive producer Stanley Mercury called, "Calsyta, knock off the shenanigans when you're delivering lines. They're baffoonish and don't cast our show in a good light."

"Really, Stanley? I read *R&R*'s ratings got a bump when I was on air. Folks like a little humor peppered into these dry-ass scripts, makes it organic, hearing stuff that reflects their own lives. Face it, Stanley, nobody talks Whitehaven."

The notorious racist had been on my back from jump. Word on the soapvine was he'd had a hand in firing every minority on both *Medical Clinic* and the soap he'd started out on, *Yesterday, Today, and Maybe Tomorrow.*

"Think what you will, Calysta. When you own your *own* soap you can write it any way you want to, but for now you're under contract with WBC and Barringer Dramatic Series. Soaps are serious business. It's called daytime *drama*, not comedy. Get it?"

"How can I not? But if you guys would just open up

the cartel a skosh, let some fresh air in the room, maybe we wouldn't be teetering on this doomsday seesaw. For the record, *Cliffhanger Weekly*'s fan-o-meter says they love my urban one-liners, so let me ask you this. . . ."

"Make it quick, Calysta, the 'five' is almost over."

"Didn't Edith once tell me that I bring in a key audience share to *R&R*?"

"Yeah, yeah, yeah, but that was . . ."

"And didn't Veronica tell you, and I quote, 'Just let Calysta rip, I trust her' after it was discovered you ate into precious production time calling your black phone-a-friend at Yale for translations after every one of my much-needed ad-libs?"

"An exaggeration."

"Sure about that? 'Cause according to Ben, you asked him what 'cooked my last grit' meant just two weeks ago when you couldn't reach your Ebonics translator. Ben was very insulted. Try to remember, just 'cause a man is brown don't mean he's black."

"Places!" shouted the stage manager.

Coolly sweeping away, I met Shannen on set, seeing we were now joined by my on-screen Valley girl daughter, Jade, and prickly pear, self-appointed grande dame Alison Fairchild Roberts.

"O-M-G! *Soap Suds Digest* put me in their crossword puzzle!" Jade exclaimed as a greeting.

Bubble-burster Alison replied, "So what, I was a clue on *Jeopardy!* last night and that's prime time. Let's shoot!"

CHAPTER 3

Bullshit . . . Bullshit . . . Bullshit . . . Me

Stealing a corner in her husband Randall's hospital room after he'd been found comatose at their premature Holmby Hills victory party, a Donna Karan-clad Alison whimpered into her cell phone to her therapist.

"You have no idea how violent those EMT people were with me. Every time I reached for Randy they pushed me back. I'm so traumatized I'm thinking about suing. Could you prescribe a sedative? I plan on staying here for as long as it takes."

The hospital door swung open to admit a battle-ax of a nurse.

"Mrs. Roberts?"

"Who wants to know? And why aren't you using my alias? I'm trying to hide from all that press downstairs," Alison slurred.

"Mrs. Roberts, it appears the press is here for Dolly Burke. I'll have to ask you to keep your voice down. We have other patients on the floor who are trying to rest," the night nurse half scolded.

Alison zigzagged her way across the room declaring, "And did you know this is a private suite and my husband is a big TV producer and I'm big too?" before plopping on Randall's bed.

Ignoring Alison's drunken rant, the nurse continued, "The doctor will be in shortly to discuss the next steps for your husband and his recovery. And I know who you are. I used to watch *The Rich and the Ruthless* when you were a stripper and I was in college, but that was a long, long, long time ago."

"Tell Doc make it snappy, I don't have all day."

The door shut.

The nurse left Alison feeling even older as she fished out Randall's ringing phone.

"Hello? Who? CiCi? Who the hell are . . . Hello?"

Click.

A belligerent Alison picked up speed rifling Randall's

pockets, hitting pay dirt in his wallet when she came across a faded, folded newspaper clipping wrapped around the yellowed Nelson-Atkins Museum of Art ID Randall nostalgically carried. Scanning the article, she grew more furious with every syllable. Though tipsy, Alison would know Beulah Espinetta Jones's hated face anywhere.

Suddenly, Randall's babbling in the ambulance about how a ". . . T.I. stole my Yacht-Master II" made sense.

"So, Calysta, this is what your backwoods homegirl had on you. My Randy knew it and *you* poisoned him to silence him." Facing the Los Angeles skyline, she avowed, "You're gonna pay, bitch, or my name isn't Alison Fairchild Roberts."

★ ★ ★

". . . or my name isn't Alison Fairchild Roberts . . . or my name isn't . . ."

"Alison, wake up, you're having a nightmare," said her acting coach, Chickie Finch.

"Huh?" Alison wiped the corner of her mouth, shaking away the unsettling memory.

"Honey, you called me to run lines. So let's hit it."

Sitting up in her chaise and taking a sip of Chablis, Alison proceeded to speed-read through the script.

"Bullshit . . . bullshit . . . bullshit . . . me. Bullshit . . . bullshit . . . bullshit . . . me. Where am I in this gawddamn script?" she griped with a clabber face, ripping out page after page, crumpling the papers before whisking them into her kidney-shaped pool accented with a mosaic *R&R* at the bottom.

"Better thank your lucky stars you still have a job, honey," reminded Chickie.

"Crucify me."

"Who am I today?" asked Chickie.

"Who else? That douche bag Wolfe . . . I mean Vidal, same difference. I swear, if casting doesn't find me a younger love interest and Veronica doesn't come up with a chunkier storyline I'm gonna find a new show."

"At fifty-eight?" challenged Chickie.

"You only know that because we grew up in the same house. Say it out loud again and you're disowned. Now, I have the first line. And do Vidal with the accent."

RORY

Vidal, darling, when do we leave for Istanbul?

Chickie dropped her voice, speaking with the worst accent ever.

VIDAL

Vhen I say so. It depends if I close the deal

vith Lady Lovekin and get back Vinn Hansen In-

ternational Biscuit Business stock she stole
from me.

RORY

I'll be seeing her today at the Whitehaven
Country Club. Why don't I have a word with her
about . . .

VIDAL

Rory, business is a man's job. Staying out of
it and keeping me happy are the only two things
you have to do.

RORY

(Tearing up)

But, Vidal, I'm only . . .

In perfect form a gorgeous, honey-toned pool boy suddenly sprang off the diving board, resurfacing with glistening skin and a devilish smile.

"Mrs. Roberts, coming in for a *deep*?"

"Not today, Micah. Got to learn my three friggin' lines. Isn't he perfect?" remarked Alison.

"Yeah, a real gem, but why's he in the pool he's supposed to be cleaning?"

"He *is* cleaning it, silly. Besides, he unlocks my pent-up passion just doing the backstroke."

"If that's all him in those trunks, I'll bet he's cleaning something else too," Chickie murmured as Micah playfully tossed a soggy paper back at Alison. "Let me know when the spitball fight is over," she said, retreating toward the bar.

"Don't be bitter, Chickie," Alison laughed. "Fix me one too."

Left unsettled by her not-a-dream, she allowed her mind to finish the scene as it had played out months earlier in the hospital.

* * *

Snatching up her own phone, she scrolled through her long list of contacts till she found Calysta Jeffries. Alison's assistant had over-helped, entering all cast and crew contact information from the *Rich and the Ruthless* Christmas card list. That Girl Friday lasted a week.

Alison slowly typed out a text to Calysta: i no wat u did 2 yr daddy, beulah.

CHAPTER 4

Bones

(MISSISSIPPI FLASHBACK)

. . . i no wat u did 2 yr daddy, beulah.

I bolted up in bed, heart hammering in my ears, drowning out the pattering rain.

"Mom, you okay?" my daughter, Ivy, questioned as she tiptoed into the bedroom. "I thought you'd be asleep, just wanted to grab my iPod."

"Fine, baby," I forced out.

"Mother Jones and Miss Whilemina cheat somethin' awful at bid whist," she teased loudly as she dug through her bag.

"Hush that mouth, chile," Grandma Jones bandied back

through the paper walls. "And don't you be stayin' up all hours with that new gadget; you have church in the mornin'."

Swallowing panic, I forced myself to lie back, gripping my phone while Ivy and Grandma Jones settled into silence.

Glancing at the message again, I saw the number was "Blocked." Who was this? Only a few people knew for certain what I'd done to my jackleg preachin' father, Chester Winslow. None of them would do this . . . except . . .

My skin went cold thinking about that snake Randall Roberts. Of course it was him. And I'd thought he'd never wake up from that coma.

* * *

After a sleepless night, I sat through eight o'clock service at Church of the Solid Rock like a zombie.

"Mom?" Ivy gently tugged my arm to steer me out. "You okay?"

"Just need some air. I'ma go for a walk," I assured, fanning myself. "I'll meet up with you at Miss Whilemina's for dinner."

The second I was out of earshot, I dialed Shannen, knowing she'd have the latest.

"Hey, Calysta, how's M–i–s–s–i–s–s–i–p–p–i?"

"Africa hot. Listen, Shan, sorry, but I gotta make this quick. I was wondering if you'd heard anything about Randall comin' out of his coma?"

"Course I did. That was weeks ago . . ."

Speechless, I picked up my jaw as Shannen continued.

"Everyone knows Veronica demoted Randall to associate producer. He's supposed to be back on set next week."

"What?"

"Javier heard Toby telling Jade, who got it from Maeve. Can't believe Randall's coming back at all!"

"Weeks ago? But, Shannen, you told me Randall was looking like a goner!"

"Well, yeah, goner from the show. . . ." She paused.

"See you when I get back, Shannen."

I hung up, mind reeling. If Randall had been out of his coma, why text me now? The juvenile message didn't seem like him. The Barringer vote was over and it wouldn't serve him to air my dirty laundry now. Surely he'd be fired, especially with Veronica planning the ultimate Ruby Stargazer clawback and counting on a ratings boost. Besides, who would believe a snake like Randall Roberts?

Gossip being the popular pastime as the church ladies prepared the baked ham, fried okra, coleslaw, field peas, skillet cornbread, and cobbler, I let the tittering waves wash over me at Miss Whilemina's.

"Did you see Doris Turner's new hat?" Miss Odile chuckled. "Pixie Ford made it . . . ugliest thing ever."

"Who could miss it?" Miss Bessie answered. "That potted plant on her head nearly knocked me down when she got up during the praise dancers' performance."

"Miss Whilemina," Ivy interrupted, "there's a man in a suit at the door asking to speak with you, said it was about a new homeowner opportunity."

"That fool? Tell him the answer's still no and I better not see *him here talkin' that mess again." Miss Whilemina slammed down the cast-iron skillet in her agitation. "Developers gettin' bolder and bolder by the second," she griped. "Come 'round here all the time sweet-talkin', tryin' to butter me up to sell my land for air puddin' and wind sauce. Nuh-uh."*

"I know that's right," Miss Bessie chimed in. "Had one come by. Told him he bettah get his thievin' hide off my property or else."

The ladies cackled.

"That's one silver linin' I got," my childhood friend Seritta said wryly. "No developers want my little ol' spot."

"Now that ain't even true," Miss Bessie corrected. "Don't think I didn't see that fat white man with the bad hair plugs come by a couple months ago."

The description caught my attention.

"What are you talkin' about?" Seritta asked, clearly confused.

"Girl, don't play. Jacob from Pride-All parked that hearse right out front my door, course I noticed."

"That's different," said Miss Odile. "Them mens usually have their own big car."

Puzzle pieces started clicking in my brain. I could hear Randall's slimy voice in my head all those weeks ago, right before the vote: "That Jacob at Pride-All is quite the tour guide."

My chest tightened. Randall had been to Greenwood, and someone helped him connect the dots with that newspaper clipping. But surely not . . . Seritta?

"I'm tellin' you, I haven't talked to no fat white man 'bout nothin'," Seritta insisted. "Maybe he spoke to my daughter."

Remembering how CiCi had looked at me at the Greenwood Barbeque Cookoff the other night, another piece clicked.

"Where's CiCi now?" I choked out.

"She in the backyard with Terrell and Pre'tentious."

* * *

Fingers snapped inches from my nose, startling me to the present.

"Don't do that!" I bit out.

"Sorry, babe, but you were somewhere else and I got things to do, places to be," said Weezi Abramowitz, my agent, manager, publicist, legal counsel, confidant, financial advisor, and escort. "Time is money."

"Yeah, mine," I retorted. "Shoulda let me daydream, you're billin' me anyway."

"You didn't hear a word I said."

"Sure I did, you'd inappropriately gone over my credit card bill again and were chastising me for staying at the Four Seasons in Beverly Hills for a week."

"Calysta, you got this big beautiful house in Malibu," Weezi said, waving his arms around. "Why spend bucks on a Beverly Hills hotel?"

"It was for someone else . . ." I started. "But why am I explaining myself to you? Is that all?"

"Nah, received a damn jury summons yesterday. Hopefully, I won't get picked but if I am, you gonna be okay without me?"

"I'm okay without you right now," I half smiled.

"Ouch," my manager tossed, grabbing his keys from the kitchen counter. "I mean it, kiddo. Be good. You just got back on this pony; don't start in with the spurs."

I traced the Four Seasons charges with my fingertips; my confrontation with CiCi in that Mississippi backyard earlier had been short and sour. That runt played dumb for two seconds before admitting she'd been the one to talk to Randall. She also shared why.

More sad than mad, I empathized with her desperation to escape the stifling life of babies and boondocks, knowing what it was like to have big dreams on a dirt road. But my compassion was tested when I asked, "Why send the text now?"

CiCi had raised her chin, saying sassily, "I wanna first-class ticket to Hollywood and sleep at that Four Seasons Hotel like dem bitches on m'show, Bad Girls be at."

I went ahead and bought that damn Delta first-class ticket and put CiCi up at the five-star hotel for a week with spending money. Why? Silence. She swore up and down she'd never speak about my secret again.

Oh yes, CiCi had herself a wild time in Hollywood, sure did. Had the nerve to show up on the *R&R* set, according to Shannen, somehow scoring an *extra* role. WBC security was still talking about it.

Seritta shared that CiCi had moved out of the trailer when she got back to Greenwood, renting her own apartment in Jackson. Didn't know how she could've afforded all that but I didn't lose sleep over it.

Though that loose end seemed to be knotted up, I still wondered just how deep you had to bury bones to keep 'em in the dirt.

CHAPTER 5

CiCi's Fifteen Minutes

A *RICH AND THE RUTHLESS* FLASHBACK

I'm sorry, miss, but I don't have a 'WBC Drive On' parking pass for you. What did you say your name was?" asked the security guard.

Irritated and smacking Bazooka in her cheap rent-a-wreck, CiCi spat, "Man, would you c'mon? It's four letters, C-I-C-I, Turner as in Ike and Tina. Bettah not make me late either," she finished, rolling her eyes and flipping the bird to the dude behind her for blaring his horn, unaware it was prime-time heartthrob Derrick Taylor.

Traffic now backed up twelve car lengths, the security guard boomed, "Miss, for the last time, you're not in the system so make a U-turn and . . ."

No sooner did the security gate rise than CiCi gunned it straight ahead, no idea where she was going, sending security into a tailspin.

"Security here. Front gate. Breach. African-American female, name: CiCi Turner, C-I-C-I, Turner as in Ike and Tina, on premises. Aggressive. Apprehend with caution. Over."

CiCi haphazardly parked behind the Deal of a Century game show studio. Slipping through an unlocked backstage door, she plucked up a yellow name tag from the floor, slapped it on her chest, and meandered through the hot tub and bedroom sets.

"Omigod, there's Monty King and his card girls saying a prayer," CiCi said to herself. "What for? Not like they need Michael Vick to score a touchdown."

"May I help you to your seat . . . um, Melissa?" asked a stage manager, eyeing the tag.

"Yes, you can." CiCi beamed as security ran past her.

* * *

After nearly getting kicked out of Deal of the Century for calling the game show host a punk ass, CiCi strode purposefully down hall-way after hallway, turning corners, taking elevators up and down to avoid security.

Stepping off on a plush-looking floor, a long hallway stretching before her, CiCi was awed by framed Rich and the Ruthless cast photos from the past thirty years, and left a trail of fingerprints and *breath marks before stepping tentatively through the* Star Trek-*ish double doors at the end.*

A pale, red-haired secretary with purple butterfly barrettes sat at her desk talking to a cute Indian dude.

"*Fern, why am I here?*" *Ben complained.*

"*Ben, you may not be where you wanna be on the soap ladder, but starting at the bottom has benefits too,*" *Fern enthused.*

"*I'm an NYU graduate,*" *he returned.* "*If I'd stayed in Bollywood—or listened to my uncle Tupe—I could've been a part of his multimillion-dollar company.*"

"*Ahem,*" *Cici fake-coughed.*

"*Hello, may I help you?*" *Fern asked.*

"*Yeah. I wanna see the set.*"

Looking at her name tag, Fern said, "*Oh . . . Melissa . . .* Deal of the Century *is . . .*"

"*Yeah, yeah, yeah, I know, just came from that tired show. I wanna see Randall Roberts. Where's the* Rich and the Ruthless *set at?*"

"*You know Randall Roberts?*" *Fern asked.*

"*Yep. And Calysta Jeffries.*"

"*I love Calysta! She plays my favorite character, Ruby Stargazer, on R&R. It wasn't the same without her. Thank God the fans never gave up!*"

"*Mm-hm,*" *CiCi said.* "*I like Emmy Abernathy m'self.*"

"*That's 'cause you don't know her,*" *Ben said snidely.* "*I'd better get back to work. Thanks for listening again, Fern.*"

"*Anytime, Ben!*"

"Well, Doris, things are pretty slow so I'll take you down to the set myself," Fern said, pulling on a knitted yellow shrug.

BARRETT

I'm warning you, Lady Lovekin, if you give Vidal back the controlling shares of Vinn Hansen International Biscuit, I'll, I'll . . . I'll . . .

GINA

You try anything sneaky, we'll make you the sorriest you've ever been, Lovekin.

LADY LESLIE

What do I look like, a friggin' idiot?

"Damn it, Maeve, that isn't your line!" Phillip burst out.

"Cut!" long-suffering R&R director Julius called.

"C'mon. That was the gist, I just gave it some spunk," Maeve Fielding, R&R's matriarch, groused. "I need a cigarette."

"Maybe you wouldn't have bronchitis every other day if you'd stop smoking," Emmy said cattily.

"And maybe people wouldn't call you a whore if you kept your underwear on."

"Who're ya callin' a whore, hag?"

"Isn't this exciting?" Fern whispered to a wide-eyed CiCi watching the heated squabble between the bubblers.

"That's five," called the stage manager.

Reaching for his flask, Julius bolted from the room wordlessly.

Ignoring Fern, CiCi ran up to the soap stars, calling, "Emmy, Emmy, you're the shit!"

Emmy spun away from Maeve, appraising CiCi's cornrows, tank top, and belly ring before gushing disingenuously, "Awww, thanks. That's so dope of you to say."

"Who's this?" Phillip sneered.

"She's a guest of Randall's or Calysta's . . . I think," Fern nervously answered.

Phillip's eyes narrowed. "Why am I not surprised? Calysta's not even here! It's bad enough she's coming back. Now she's inviting her overurbanized homies here too," he fumed.

"Excuse you, you ain't much of nothin' ya own damn self," CiCi snapped, getting in Phillip's face. "And Vidal's gonna kick your punk ass when he finds out about your shady biscuit deal. And why you always gotta be up in Justine's Kool-Aid? Ain't nobody thinkin' 'bout your butt."

Instantly cowed by the petite pit bull, Phillip turned and bolted.

"Oh dear, I'm sorry about that," Fern apologized, steering CiCi into the control booth. Taking in the wall of TV screens, lighted buttons, and knobs, CiCi was mesmerized.

"Mr. Roberts! I'm so glad you're back," Fern exclaimed.

CiCi took in Randall's shocked face as he placed her.

*   *   *

"You don't understand," Randall hissed at CiCi in an R&R utility closet. Knowing he had a knotty problem on his hands, he continued, "I don't have the power I used to on the soap to hire you."

"Look, you promised me in Mississippi. 'Gimme a call when ya get to town,' 'member? Well I'm in town, big as day, and you bettah not be renegin'."

"It's impossible," Randall pleaded.

CiCi didn't reply.

Wrongly sensing weakness, Randall continued, "I just suffered a major health scare. I almost died. And . . ."

"Man, save it for your mamma, folks die every day," CiCi said dismissively. "Get me one of them 'background' parts and twenty K, and we'll be straight."

"Twenty . . ." He couldn't even finish.

"Pawn some shit. Twenty K ain't nothin' to you. And don't think I forgot about that background part. I wanna go home and say I was on TV. Just once." For a moment CiCi's face softened into the dreaming child she used to be.

Before Randall could exploit the moment it passed, CiCi's shell hardening again.

"You can be in the next scene, I'll arrange it."

Whitehaven Diner. We see Dove, Jade, and Toby in a red-vinyl booth, in conversation.

DOVE

Remember, your mother's been lost at sea almost

a year; seems impossible she could've survived

that fall off the yacht.

JADE

(Emotional, lots of tears)

Like, I know that, Dad. But we can't stop

searching.

AXEL

Jade's right, man. I don't remember Ruby since

I hit my head driving my Harley off Whitehaven

Quarry, but Jade tells me her mom was a really

strong swimmer. And I totally think—

"CUT!" Julius yelled. "That extra is WAVING AT THE CAMERA."

"Calm down, Julius," said a sweating Randall.

"That's five," said the stage manager.

"Wait, we have to reshoot the scene, that extra was staring into the friggin' camera," Julius spat.

"You know Veronica's new rule," said Randall with a shrug. "Whatever plays stays. Audience won't notice."

Pulling his hair, Julius stalked out of the control booth.

CiCi sidled up to Randall. "I was good, huh?"

* * *

Settling back into her plush first-class seat, CiCi ordered a rum and Coke from the flight attendant. She opened her purse and gazed satisfactorily at the thick wad of cash.

"I'm a rich bitch," she repeated to herself.

CHAPTER 6

Business Behind
the Bubbles

*W*eezi's warning words stuck in my head the next day. No doubt he was remembering our less-than-successful first contract meeting with Edith Norman, negotiating the terms of my return to the soap. Despite Veronica's mediating presence, the WBC president of daytime was determined to ignore my worth to *The Rich and the Ruthless*, offering a pittance of a salary.

"You know that word *servitudinous*?" I'd asked.

"I don't think that's a word, Calysta," snapped Edith.

"It is now. It means working indefinitely for squat—"

"Let's revisit the offer so that it reflects Calysta's value, her talent, what she brings to the WBC and Barringer table," Weezi interrupted, smoothing feathers.

"This shouldn't even be an issue."

"Okay, Calysta, I'll handle this," Weezi stressed.

"I ain't here to watch paint dry. They'll call us when they're ready to have a real meeting."

Weezi trailed out after me, purple.

I shook my head replaying the incident. It was a fine line to walk, keeping change movin' forward without getting kicked to the curb, but as much as Weezi preferred I keep my mouth shut, he knew he'd just have to let me do me. 'Cause I don't pander, baby, not even for a contract.

Stagehands were busy swapping out walls, art, and an assortment of props, while Maeve yelled craggily, "Where's wardrobe, these damn Ferragamos are killing my corns. Get me some Dr. Scholl's or I'm wearin' my Payless."

"I have your pads and your Depends," muttered Penelope, *R&R*'s abused wardrobe mistress, known by all as the Pattern Cutter, sweeping by me.

"Dollar for your thoughts," a low, sexy voice sounded at my side.

Startled, I turned to find the new assistant director, Max Gardner, his gray eyes dancing with amusement as he studied me. Six foot, tanned, ink-dark hair, five o'clock shadow over a chiseled chin, he was sex on a stick and my body radar was in overdrive.

"A whole dollar?" I flirted. "Flattered you put such a high premium on my thoughts."

Leaning in, adding instant intimacy, he extended a strong hand to take one of mine, giving it a lingering shake. "Max Gardner. Heard a lot about you."

"Calysta Jeffries," I replied, back on guard. "Don't believe everything you hear."

"I read between the lines," he said, instantly setting me at ease.

This was a first. I gave him a head-to-toe appraisal—noticing his Hambidge T-shirt and jeans complimenting his strong lean body. His intelligent eyes intrigued me, but it was that hint of mystery that really drew me in.

"Done checking me out?" he teased.

"I'm not—" I started.

"Too bad," he said, cutting me off good-naturedly.

Feeling my face heat, I covered, "Hambidge?" indicating his T-shirt.

"Got it at Goodwill."

"So how's it feel to be the new assistant director?" I asked.

"Feel a whole lot better if you told me we could be friends."

"Max, my name is Calysta Pay-My-Own-Bills Jeffries. Slow your roll."

Mischievousness covered his face. "What can I say? I go after what I want and usually get it."

Torn between intense attraction and knee-jerk caution, I took a few steps back.

"Get to know me before you make any final decisions. Dinner?" He smiled irresistibly.

Couldn't help but laugh at his shameless charm.

Max swept up my hand, planting a soft kiss on the back of it before striding off. A frisson coursed through my body, leaving me hot.

Running over, grabbing my arm, Shannen asked, "What was that?"

"What was what?"

"The eye sex between you and Max?"

"Don't be silly."

"Mm-hm, whatever," she said. "I know chemistry when I see it. You should definitely hit that equipment, Calysta. He's total man candy."

"Girl, you're crazy," I said, laughing. "Gotta get ready for my next scene."

Maybe some things stayed the same, but when things got different they got interesting. And things just got very different on *The Rich and the Ruthless*.

* * *

Seated on the terrace of the popular Hollywood eatery Cabana was Edith Norman and soap opera industry miscreant Stanley Mercury. Blossom Dearie crooned in the distance.

Stanley had been hired on to *The Rich and the Ruthless* for his henchman skills more than producing acumen. He'd made no secret about preferring his soap opera landscapes lily white, once quoted as saying, "Now that Willie Turner and folks like that are off the show we no longer have to cater to poor people." That quote got Stanley fired from *Yesterday, Today, and Maybe Tomorrow* and it wouldn't be his last pink slip for unsavory remarks and behavior. He'd been unemployable for a good decade since, let go from *Medical Clinic* after producers saw him on CNN in a march in Alabama, replete with swastikas and Confederate flags.

"Would you care for something to drink?" asked the gorgeous waiter.

"Lemonade," ordered Edith.

"Bourbon on the rocks," growled Stanley.

She zeroed in on Stanley.

"You've been getting rave reviews from the cast and crew, with the exception of Javier and Calysta."

"That Mexican's horrible," scoffed Stanley.

"Who cares? He brings in a record audience share. No one else even comes close. Javier's appeal with advertisers is through the roof. We'd never have La Tienda: 'Share the Flavors of Spain' as a main sponsor or a deal with Telemundo if it weren't for Javier."

"Fine, I'll take it easy on him."

"Knew you'd understand. I want you to call him and apologize."

"For what?"

"For being heavy-handed. Ask Javier for his advice, how you could be a better producer. I think . . ."

"You're losing it, Edith. Besides, we should be talking about Calysta and how I can knock that black bitch off her perch," Stanley sneered.

"Keep your voice down, will you? Diversity is huge right now in Hollywood. If we bring any attention to her in a negative light too soon we'll have more than *Cliffhanger Weekly* asking questions. The last thing we need is Al Sharpton showing up in front of the WBC network."

Stanley nodded grudgingly. "In that case, guess all I have to do is get your butthead actors to act."

"That's right, Chicken Little," said Edith with a warning smile. "Just because pretty boy Javier can't act his way out of a paper bag and Calysta is back with her big mouth doesn't mean the sky is falling."

"Your drinks," announced the waiter. "Your lunch orders?"

"Iceberg wedge, hold the blue, no croutons," piped Edith. "Sir?"

"Another bourbon and a burger, let it bleed." Turning back to Edith: "Maybe we can't do anything too obvious to Calysta but we can approach the problem from another angle," Stanley said, calculating.

"And that's exactly why I hired you," Edith said shrewdly. "What did you have in mind?"

Reaching into his leather briefcase he pulled out last month's *Soap Suds Digest* with Calysta Jeffries on the cover; the headlining story read: "Ruby Stargazer Rises from Her

Watery Grave!" Flipping to a dog-eared page, he opened it to an 'At Home' feature. His stubby finger pointed at Calysta's face and her beautiful young daughter, Ivy, at their Malibu home. "Read this," he grunted.

The snippet read: "Calysta with her teenage daughter, Ivy. A budding actress in her own right, Ivy recently starred in her high school play and hinted she might be interested in following in her mother's legendary footsteps. Does Calysta approve? 'I'm wary of Ivy entering this business,' she admits. 'But of course I'll support my baby if that's what she really wants.'"

"What am I looking at?" Edith snapped, scanning the article.

"A younger, prettier, more impressionable version of Calysta," Stanley said deviously. "Or should I say . . ."

"A controllable version," Edith finished, insect eyes lighting up behind her tortoiseshell glasses.

"Mother-daughter competition," Stanley added with a satisfied nod. "Let's see how secure Calysta is when she's set against her own flesh and blood for the limelight. Any luck, the kid'll be a hit and we'll just sit back and watch the shit hit the fan. We know the *R&R* audience doesn't accept just anyone new on the show, but Calysta Jeffries' own daughter? Fans'll eat it up."

"What if the kid tanks?" Edith asked bluntly.

"Fire her," Stanley said dismissively, as the waiter arrived with another Four Roses and lunch. "And if Calysta opens her big mamma mouth to defend her 'baby,' we'll fire her too—again. Either way it means ratings for us."

"You're going to do very well, Stanley. And let's not bring that schmuck Randall into the fold."

"Why would I?"

Edith gave Stanley a rueful smile before toasting, "Here's to bringing that bitch down."

RUH-ROH, KIDDOS, LOOKS LIKE IT'S NOT JUST THE BROADS HAVING "TROUBLE COMMUNICATING" ON THE RICH AND THE RUTHLESS *SET.* The guys are getting in on the action too! In the first ring we have the soap czar himself, Wolfe Hudson (spotted recently at Le Cirque in New York chatting up a gaggle of Trump models following the Victoria's Secret fashion show, ordering bubbly and Blue Point oysters for all. Hey, big spender!) versus debonair divo Phillip McQueen, who's none too happy that Wolfe's surprising rekindled romance storyline with bubblette Shannen Lassiter is encroaching on his current front burner love triangle and receiving sizzling Sudsy Award prenom buzz. According to a super soap set snitch, police were called in yesterday after a bubble brawl broke out with Wolfe butch-slapping Phillip silly! To your corners, gentlemen!

In the second ring, we have demoted (ouch) associate producer Randall Roberts versus new co-exec producer Stanley Mercury. Tension is running Kilimanjaro high as Randall works on regaining his former seat, while Stanley's already dug his claws in deep on *R&R*. Check in with secretsofasoapoperadiva.com to see who winds up on top and who gets KO'd!

The Diva

CHAPTER 7

Old Dogs, New Tricks

At a car wash on Sunset Boulevard, Randall waited for his leased Mercedes as an old West Indian put the final touches on his Guccis. He'd confided in the shoe-shine man like a therapist about his most recent fight with wifey, Alison. It'd been about money again, their only topic of conversation since he was discharged from the hospital.

"Alison," he'd pleaded. "I can only make so much in this pathetic position. You know I'm working as hard as I can to get my job back from that jerk Stanley."

"Well you better make it UPS snappy," Alison had hissed.

"'Cause we have two mortgages, a yacht, and a whole lotta other debt."

"Maybe if you cut out the Brazilian sculpting procedures," he'd muttered.

Randall rubbed his forehead where the Zane romance novel she'd thrown had hit after his comment.

What Alison didn't know about their current money woes was that Randall, after some dark weeks following waking up in the hospital, had pulled himself together and taken a major, if risky, step toward rebuilding his fortune and regaining his full claim on *The Rich and the Ruthless.*

Determined to pull himself up the slippery soap ladder by any means necessary while drowning in debt—thanks to a dramatic pay cut, blackmail money paid to CiCi Turner, and a boatload of other bills—Randall revisited a highly lucrative trade he'd dabbled in decades ago: art forgery.

"Womens crazy, Mr. Roberts," the shoeshine man commented. "You know what they say, can't live with them . . . the end."

Randall gave the man a tiny tip as he stepped down, leaving the copy of *Cliffhanger Weekly* behind. The cover declared, "Shake-ups at *R&R*! Mystery Cast Addition?!"

Irate he didn't know anything about new casting, Randall slid into his Mercedes and peeled out toward the WBC studio.

In Izod, khakis, and topsiders, he trotted down to set to put in more face time with the cast. Jaw clenched, Randall spotted the man who made his eyes water with fury.

"Ah, Stanley, just the man I wanted to see," Randall greeted.

"What do you want, Roberts, I'm busy."

"Any truth to that *Cliffhanger Weekly* story?" Randall asked.

"You don't have to worry about that," Stanley tossed to him as he tried to pass. "Why don't you go up to your office and rest?"

Randall sidestepped, blocking Stanley's path. The two men stood glaring face-to-face.

"Outta my way, Randall."

"Or what?"

The pudgy, middle-aged men squared off like gunslingers.

"Or I'm going to make you," Stanley asserted.

"I'd like to see you try."

Not taking the bait, Stanley said, "Knock it off, Roberts, I don't want to hurt a defenseless—"

"Sorry to bother you, Stanley," an upset Shannen interrupted, "but I need some clarity around this new love triangle. One of the writers said Pepe and Justine are gonna break up for good! That can't be true."

Stanley wheeled away from Randall, biting out, "Yes, Shannen, the audience is having trouble seeing you string along three men. The network got a lot of hate mail about you cavorting with a minority on camera. Besides, the fans love you with Wolfe and your ongoing relationship with . . .

with . . . What the devil is Phillip's blasted name on the soap?" he asked with a clenched fist, stamping his foot.

"Barrett Fink," Shannen desperately reminded him.

"Yes, how could I forget? Barrett Fink. He can't be touched."

"But the audience loves seeing Shannen have sex with Javier more," Randall interrupted. "If we're cutting someone it should be Phillip. No one cares about that pairing anymore."

"Yeah," Shannen agreed. "Plus I love working with Javier."

"Yes, I know," Stanley retorted.

"Besides, why am I always the one who has to flip-flop between all the guys on the soap anyway? It's so slutty and unnatural."

"Don't be shortsighted, Shannen, you're so convincing. Can't put a price on uncompromising sex appeal. Now run along," Stanley said, dismissing her.

Blinking back tears, Shannen swallowed her disappointment and exited.

Putting their previous spat on the back burner, Randall continued, "Why are you squashing one of the few storylines giving us headlines? Does Veronica know about this?"

"Veronica's a busy girl," Stanley said, grinding his heels in further. "Producing, writing, taking care of family matters—that's why she hired me. Clearly, she knew *you* were incompetent."

"You friggin' douche bag," Randall growled. "If you think I'm going to let you walk in here and steal a *job for life* from me, you're—"

"Spare me, Roberts, you've got no sway," Stanley said, brushing him off, checking his watch, "and I have an important meeting with a promising young actress. Ciao."

Ducking around corners like a third-rate spy, Randall dogged Stanley right up until he stepped into what used to be his old office. Just as the door clicked shut Randall spotted the back of a tall, chicly dressed girl, Stanley greeting her warmly.

Beating a hasty retreat back down to the control booth, Randall picked up the phone.

DOVE

I don't feel right about talking to you about this business merger, Mr. Vinn Hansen. I'm faithful to Barrett Fink and . . .

VIDAL

No one's asking you to betray your boss. On the contrary, my boy, this information vould help him achieve more in the vorld. As I've explained to your beautiful vife, Ruby, this is an opportunity for you both as vell.

RUBY

Listen to the boss man, Dove, honey.

~~Yeah, Dove, I really think we should~~

Vidal's lookin' out for us.

~~listen to what Vidal has to say about~~

~~this. It seems like he wants what is~~

~~best for us.~~

VIDAL

Oh, Ruby, it's good to have you back in Vhite-

haven and not lost in the African jungle.

"CUT," Julius yelled hoarsely. "Randall called; we're shooting off the damn set again. He can see the extras knitting and doing crossword puzzles in the background. Let's add in the wall with the artsy-fartsy Man-Et stuff and a bookcase, stage left."

"Manet?" Max remarked lazily from his chair in the booth. "Why so specific?"

"I'm not paid enough to keep track or care," Julius said, taking a hit off his flask.

"Okay, guys, take five," the stage manager called.

"Calysta, excellent trimming of zose clunky lines. It's striking how you can tell vhen Felicia sneaks her veakness into Veronica's scripts."

Dashing Danish bubbler Wolfe Hudson was my favorite costar besides Shannen and I was thrilled to finally have scenes with him in a plot I'd consulted on.

Burly stagehands rolled the wall into place behind us, stabilizing it with sandbags.

"Okay, Julius, we're set," the stage manager reported. Pickin' it up right where we left off."

CHAPTER 8

Un Clavo Saca El Otro ("One Nail Drives Out the Other")

FRANCISCA

O, Juan, te amo tanto . . .

JUAN

O, Francisca, no quiero vivir sin tu . . .

ROSA

(Bursting through the door)

Vete al infierno, Juan. Es un desgraciado, Francisca. ¡La estado estafando a usted con Melinda, te lo juro!

> **JUAN**
>
> *(Grabbing Rosa roughly)*
>
> *¡Cállate!*
>
> **ROSA**
>
> *(Struggling)*
>
> *¡No me toques, estúpido!*
>
> **FRANCISCA**
>
> *¡Ay, dios mío, Juan, no!*
>
> **JUAN**
>
> *Francisca, yo te prometo—*
>
> **ROSA**
>
> *Tengo prueba, amigo! Las imagenes . . .*
>
> **FRANCISCA**
>
> *(Throwing herself onto the plush velvet chaise,*
>
> *weeping uncontrollably)*
>
> *¡Lárgate, Juan! ¡Nunca quiero verte jamás!*
>
> **JUAN**
>
> *(Glaring menacingly at Rosa)*
>
> *Te voy a matar!*

Drawn by my daughter Ivy's fits of giggles, I walked into our living room to find Javier Vásquez's handsome face glaring at me from the television, the camera holding on his face longer than necessary. Ivy was lounging on the couch, a bowl of popcorn balanced on her lap.

"What are you watching?" I asked.

"That telenovela Javier stars on," she answered through laughter.

"Why?"

"It's so over-the-top hilarious. I mean, I have no idea what they're saying but I can totally follow the emotion of it. Plus, it's good research."

"Research for . . ."

"Acting," she said nonchalantly.

I worked to keep my face from falling.

"Don't know if that's really the best acting research but you'll certainly learn drama. Now come on, your grandma Jones is on the phone and wants to wish you a happy birthday."

Ivy muted the show and jumped up, skipping past me to the kitchen. I mulled over her words. It worried me, Ivy's increasing interest in acting. Naturally, I'd support her in whatever she wanted to do, but I wanted something a little less venomous for my daughter than the showbiz snake pit. Unfortunately, it seemed the acting bug had bit and my daughter was approaching it as she did everything she set her mind to, head-on with unshakable focus.

Drifting into the kitchen, I heard Ivy pipe, "Of course I'm going to college, Grandma, but there's an amazing job opportunity that I'd be crazy to pass up. I'll let you know the second I know for sure."

I watched Ivy say her good-byes and "I love yous," turning to me as she hung up the phone.

"Hey, Mom," she said with a lilt, "is it time for cake?"

"You know it," I said, trying to stem my concern.

Officially, it was Ivy's milestone eighteenth birthday and our time to celebrate; we'd ordered in Thai and I'd baked her two-layer red velvet cake myself. She was legal—sort of. Boy, was that a scary thought. Tomorrow she'd be going out with friends.

I counted out eighteen candles and lit them, carrying the cake to the table. Ivy turned off the kitchen lights, and her sweet face lit up as I set the confection down in front of her.

"Oh, Mom, thank you, it's perfect!"

"I love you, Ivy. Make a wish and blow out those candles before they start drippin' wax."

It was déjà vu watching the dancing flames glow in my daughter's beautiful face, her lips whispering wishes into the candlelight. Déjà vu but with a sad newness—she was eighteen. Where had the time gone?

"Happy birthday, sweetheart."

She gave me a kiss on the cheek before turning on the lights and cutting us each a big piece.

"Mmmm, it's so good!" she exclaimed as she took another forkful.

I took a tiny bite, calculating how many sessions with my trainer it would take to work off the whole piece.

Unable to extinguish my growing worry any longer, I asked, "Honey, what's this amazing job you were talking to Grandma Jones about?"

"Oh that," she said, taking her time to swallow. "It's a really cool opportunity."

"In addition to college?"

"Instead of . . ." Cutting off my protest she added quickly, ". . . for now. I'm still going, just . . . taking a gap year."

"That amazing, huh?" I asked, working to keep my voice light.

"Just a job," she said, evading the issue. "But kind of a once-in-a-lifetime thing. It'll be awesome, and you're gonna be super proud of me."

"Why so secretive?" I pressed.

"Oh, Mom, let me surprise you," she said playfully. "You'll find out really, really soon. Promise."

*   *   *

I lost sleep over Ivy's mystery career path but had to put it out of my mind once I arrived at work the next day.

"Where's Javier?" professional whiner Phillip demanded. "I've been ready for twenty minutes. According to the company memo we're on a tight schedule."

"We are," grumbled Julius, "but Javier got held up on *Mi Amor, Mi Odio* so we have to shoot around him."

"This is ridiculous. I can't take that nonprofessional one more sec—"

"Phillip, if you had two shows we'd do the same for you," Julius dryly stated.

"Attention, everyone." Stanley Mercury stomped onto set. "Attention."

Scooting out of his direct line of vision, I ended up in Max's. He gave me a wink.

"C'mon, let's not move like a herd of turtles. Gather 'round quickly, I have exciting news."

The cast shuffled closer.

"You're givin' us back the money you stole in those outrageous pay cuts?" Maeve cawed.

"No," Stanley snapped.

"We're getting vacation pay?" Ethan chimed in hopefully.

"Stop guessing!" Stanley spat, glancing dismissively at Randall. "I'm pleased to say our *Rich and the Ruthless* family will be expanding."

"What?" Alison shrieked. "I better not be gettin' a kid or so help me—"

"Quiet, Alison, let the man finish," I cautioned.

"In fact, *you,* Calysta, will be especially happy about this addition." Stanley smiled.

"Oh?"

He turned to motion someone from behind the duvetyn curtain.

"Everyone give a warm welcome to our newest *Rich and the Ruthless* cast member."

Amid the applause, I stood frozen as my daughter, Ivy, stepped out onto the soundstage beaming. "Surprise, Mom!"

Catching my breath, I rushed forward and hugged Ivy, kissing her on both cheeks. Some costars made no secret of their resentment, while Shannen, Wolfe, and Toby greeted Ivy enthusiastically, Toby a little too enthusiastically. I'd have to keep my eye on that one.

Internally, I was devastated.

CHAPTER 9

A Change Could Do You Good

*B*reathe, girl, can't be that bad." Derrick Taylor's silky voice did little to calm my nerves as I paced in heeled slippers, scarfing Haagen-Dazs, as he reclined on my California king. "Come on ovah here and let me . . ."

"Derrick, I didn't call you over for that. . . ." I said. "I need to talk. . . ."

"You need to let a brotha relieve all that tension Flow-master style," he said suggestively, unbuttoning his Armani shirt halfway.

"Would you be serious? Those sneaky execs back-doored

Ivy onto *R&R* behind my back. You know they're up to somethin'."

"Weren't you the one talkin' 'bout diversity? Could be they're finally listenin'. Plus, Ivy's cute, got skills," Derrick said dismissively, propping himself on an elbow, flexing a bicep. "When you called sayin' you needed to talk I didn't know you meant actually 'talk.' You gonna slip between these Egyptians with me or what?"

"Stop playin', D. You know how difficult this business is; it'll ruin my baby. I've always protected Ivy—"

"And maybe she feels suffocated, wants to fly the coop, get her own crib. You know . . . be independent."

"But this industry will chew her up and . . ."

"Think you're underestimatin' her. She *is* your daughter after all."

"Yes, but that doesn't mean she can *do* this kind of work. It takes a certain . . . a certain . . . kind of grit," I exhaled.

"Didn't you say she was doin' plays and stuff?" he sighed, sitting up, rebuttoning his shirt.

"Pfttt, school plays, gimme a break," I said, waving the words away with my spoon. "I'm talkin' *daytime drama*; thousands of lines to memorize, people and circumstances to navigate. It's an entirely different world and not one you can just float into on a magic carpet of nepotism."

Derrick's low chuckle interrupted me. "You think you might be gettin' a little too worked up? Is this only about Ivy? Besides, you'd be surprised what she's probably learned already, coming to set all these years, watchin' you and everyone else; hours of rehearsals, running lines with you, listening to all the tales. I wouldn't be surprised if Ivy hits that stage and takes all y'all by storm. Let's face it, Calysta, it ain't that hard."

"But she's only eighteen," I bemoaned melodramatically between spoonfuls, "she's just a *baby*."

"And how old were you when you left Greenwood? Didn't you tell me you were seventeen?"

"Those were desperate circumstances. Besides, age is not the point. I'm hurt that she didn't even discuss joining *R&R* with me beforehand. Bottom line, I'm her mother! And Ivy's always known she could tell me anything."

"She wanted to surprise you. . . ."

"Oh, I'm surprised all right."

* * *

A week later I was still grappling with the fact that Edith and Stanley had hired my daughter in some weird form of sabotage.

When I'd spoken to Veronica about it, she'd admitted she must've signed off on the hiring, but had been so distracted by other mounting concerns on the show she didn't see a problem with it.

"Ivy's your daughter, Calysta, I'm sure she'll be wonderful. And if showbiz interests her, what a fantastic opportunity, don't you think?"

"Maybe, but, Veronica, don't you find it a tad suspicious?"

"To be honest, Calysta, I don't. As much as I'd like to be on set more I simply can't. The business of running our soaps is all-consuming. Plus, between helping my mom keep an eye on my brother and my father's recovery, I'm exhausted."

"Of course you are. I'm sorry, I should've asked earlier, how is your dad?"

"Getting stronger every day," she reassured me. "Listen, Calysta, I do have to put some trust into Stanley's hands."

"I understand."

"According to Felicia, Ivy's going to interact quite a bit with your character, isn't that wonderful?"

Maybe. I was sure that wasn't Stanley and Edith's endgame. Interestingly, Randall seemed to be the only other person as concerned about the casting as I was.

Across the set, I watched Ivy and Toby rehearse. She looked so sophisticated in full makeup, hair pulled back in a sleek chignon, wearing an off-the-shoulder Marchesa dress. Wonder what happened to the oh-so-tight clothing budget the Pattern Cutter was always reminding *me* about.

"You okay?"

I knew the voice and didn't dare turn around.

"Fine," I lied. Why did he always catch me off guard?

"Want to talk about it?"

"Talk about what?"

Max touched my shoulder, turned me to face him, then

gave me a knowing look. "I'm not blind, I can see having your daughter here is bothering you somehow."

"You don't know what you're talking about."

His eyes shifted to a giggling Ivy as she walked across the set with Toby, who had one arm draped over her shoulders, whispering in her ear.

Max's restraining hand stopped me before I could start.

"Handle it at home," he suggested.

"And observant too," I said.

"Only when I care. Sure you don't want to talk about it?"

"Not sure of anything anymore."

"How 'bout dinner t'morrow night?" he suggested.

It took me three heartbeats to repeat, "Dinner tomorrow night."

CHAPTER 10

"Love Is a Battle, Love Is a War; Love Is a Growing Up"

—JAMES BALDWIN

*Y*ou're going on a date with that cute assistant director?" Ivy smirked from behind me.

"How'd you hear about that?" I asked, trying to read her reflection in my vanity mirror as I clasped my diamond Tiffany hoops.

"Toby heard it from Javier, and Javier heard it from Shannen," she recited.

"Help me with this, honey, will you?"

Ivy zipped up my Hervé Léger bandage dress. "You know gossip spreads like wildfire on set, Mom."

"Yes, I know, I've only been there seventeen years longer than you," I said a tad too sharply.

Ivy put her hands up in surrender, pirouetting back to my bed, kicking off her bebe boots, flopping spread-eagle across the silk duvet comforter. "Seriously, Max is total man candy, but what about Derrick?"

"Don't say 'man candy,' you got that from Shannen," I half scolded, giving her a side glance.

Ivy shrugged.

"Derrick and I . . . we're, um . . . complicated. Let's not talk about him right now." I took in the formfitting mini-dress and patterned tights Ivy was sporting and asked, "You goin' out?"

"Yeah, Toby's taking me to a party."

"You're not going to any party with that no-account Toby and his rough 'n' ready friends. Gawd only knows what would happen."

Ivy sat up, stubbornness replacing her smile.

"Nothing will happen, Mom, it's just a party. Besides, I have to go, I'm the guest of honor; Toby's throwing it to welcome me to the show and introduce me to kids more my own age. It would be a disaster if I flaked. Maybe Toby is a whole bowl of crazy but I like him . . . a lot. I can handle myself. Just need you to trust me on this. Okay?"

I crossed to sit beside my defiant child.

"Honey, you know when I was in Tranquility Tudor, Toby was there too, and . . ."

"He's clean now," she defended, cutting in.

"He got kicked out," I finished. "It was his sixth rehab. Toby's not an evil boy but he's got issues. Not to mention he needs his toes to count. I don't want to see you get mixed up with him."

"Mom, I'm still the sensible girl you raised. I'm not gonna do anything dumb. Give me some credit. Toby's fun, he makes me laugh. Some of the *R&R* cast will be there too."

"Really? Like who?" I asked, feeling a skosh alienated.

"Well, like, Jade."

"That doesn't make me feel any better, Ivy. She has a monster eating disorder—chews her food and spits it out and doesn't care who's watching—to stay a size zero."

"So . . . ? Shannen and Javier said they might drop by too."

Knowing Shannen, I doubted she'd stop by any party of Toby's, but I held my tongue. I could see Ivy was going whether I officially gave her permission or not.

"Promise you'll be home by one a.m., no drinking and driving."

"Mom . . ." Ivy sighed.

Taking my silence as acquiescence, she jumped up, grabbing her boots, saying, "I promise. You keep forgetting I'm the daughter you raised," and winked, ducking out of the room. Yes, she was. Just didn't know if I found that comforting or not.

* * *

"You look really beautiful," Max said for a second time as we drove up Pacific Palisades.

"Thanks again," I replied, checking out his relaxed threads, the top three buttons of his shirt undone. Away from the set he wasn't so cocksure of himself; I liked that I made him nervous. He'd been ten minutes early to pick me up, driving a silver Prius, the Brand New Heavies playing.

"It's a rental," he'd said.

He'd made reservations at Geoffrey's in Malibu, one of my favorite spots. Perched on the hillside, our candlelit table on the flower-filled patio offered a spectacular view of the curving coastline.

"Would you care for a Shiraz or Merlot this evening?" the movie-star-looking waiter asked.

"No, thanks, pomegranate juice, with a splash of club soda, please."

"Certainly, and for you, sir?"

"Glass of Cabernet."

"Very good."

"I hope this place is okay," Max said as the waiter left.

"One of my favorites," I assured him. "I always order the same thing."

"Good. I'm more a homebody, steak-and-fries kinda guy."

"Hey, we coulda gone to Roscoe's Chicken and Waffles and I woulda been set." I smiled.

"I've never taken out a famous woman before. I wanted to make an impression," he said smoothly, his raven hair ruffling in the Pacific breeze. "So how's it feel to be back on set?"

"That's quite the non sequitur," I said lightly. "It's . . . different. Still extremely competitive."

"More so now that your daughter is on the show?"

"It's an adjustment."

As the waiter set down our drinks, Max asked, indicating the menu, "Calysta . . . ?"

"The grilled ahi."

"I'll take that prime Kobe with fries," Max finished, standing up to remove his jacket, asking, "May I sit next to you?"

"Ah, sure," I said, caught off guard. My olfactory receptors caught his spicy cologne as he nestled in.

"Was that Randall Roberts's decision? Hiring Ivy? Heard there's no love lost between you and that he's not the easiest guy to get along with."

"You heard right," I said as I took a sip and slid back. "But it wasn't Randall's decision. It was all Stanley Mercury, another thorn in my side. Last thing Randall wants is another Jeffries on set."

"That a fact?" Max asked, studying me.

"Are we really sitting in one of the most romantic spots on the planet talking about Randall Roberts and Stanley Mercury?"

Max looked down shamefaced. "I was just tryin' to . . ."

Dinner arrived and I waited for the waiter to clear before replying, "Talkin' shop's okay, but Stanley and Randall are deadly for my digestion."

Max gave a thoughtful nod as he took a bite. "Yeah, they're both scumbags. Guess Edith Norman got the perfect person to fill in for Roberts."

"Scumbag shouldn't be a prerequisite to be a producer on *The Rich and the Ruthless*," I said. "Veronica thought Edith was making a good decision tappin' Stanley. Truth is he's ten times worse than Randall."

"You close with Veronica?"

"She's been supportive."

"Barringers close with Randall?"

"Wouldn't say close."

"Awful forgivin' of them to demote that con artist instead of firing him," Max stated.

"There's a lot of history between . . . Wait, we're talking too much shop again," I said.

"You're right."

"Let's talk about you," I suggested. "I hardly know anything about you."

"Not lots to know," he said. "Single, no kids, like to read, hike, take road trips on my Harley. Your turn."

"Wait. Where are you from?"

"I'm an army brat . . . everywhere. Your turn," Max repeated, leaning in.

"Me? Um . . ." I hesitated, "I'm a Southern belle."

"Likes, dislikes, turn-ons . . ." He grinned wickedly, reaching his arm across the back of my chair.

My adrenaline surged. Okay, it's way too soon for anything but candles, dinner, and eye sex. Breathe. "Likes: popping bubble wrap, old movies, and the Celtics. Dislikes: Randall Roberts, Stanley Mercury, and cigarette smoke."

"Anything else," Max pried.

"I love bubble baths and sitting by the ocean with a handsome, mysterious man who rides a Harley. That certainly counts as a turn-on," I said flirtatiously.

His eyes melted me as he slid his fingers through mine. "Lucky me."

★　★　★

Three hours later, Max and I twirled into my living room locked in a tight embrace. Seriously, I hadn't intended on inviting him in, but fevered by the need for affection and after the deep, chemical kiss he laid on me at the door, I couldn't resist.

Max slid his strong hand down the curve of my spine to cup my bottom. Matching his lust, I pressed against his impressive impression, yankin' off his jacket before grippin' his muscular shoulders to pull him down onto the couch. He didn't skip a beat; pressin' me back into the cushions, stretchin' his hard body on top of mine, a hot hand slidin' down the length of my thigh, then under my dress.

"Max," I gasped.

He laid another steamy kiss on me.

"I think . . . we should . . . go someplace more comfortable," Max whispered, tracin' more kisses along my jaw, headin' south.

"Nng-kay," I mumbled from the crook of his neck. *Or we could stay right here.*

I untucked his shirt and *pop, pop, pop* went the rest of his buttons. *Jackpot!* I thought to myself, running my hands over his smooth, muscular back. He really was all brawn, leaner than Derrick but no less thick.

We were just about to get me unzipped when the front door flew open, followed by the sound of Ivy's muffled laughter. She had company too.

Max and I scrambled apart, pulling ourselves together as my daughter stumbled into the living room with Toby.

"Ivy!" I tugged my dress down farther, smoothing my hair. Seeing my daughter tripping over herself clearly drunk doused my *désir charnel* like a bucket of cold water.

"Momm, ohhh man, I di'int know you'd ssstill be up," she slurred, laughing, holding on to Toby like a lamppost.

"Hey dude, we're gonna party on. Ivy says it's cool if I crash 'ere," he said with a stupid glazed smile.

"What the hell? You promised you wouldn't drink, that you'd call if you needed me to come get you," I said, stalking over to grab Ivy away from him.

"Chill, mom," Ivy slurred, then refocused on Max.

"Heyyy, whus goin' on herr? Whoo-hooo, go, Mom!" She giggled, sliding to the couch.

"Way to hook it up, man, top shelf, top shelf," Toby added, holding his fist out for a bump.

Max crossed to Toby and gently but firmly took his arm, steering him toward the door. "You need to go, man. Can't believe you were behind a wheel. I'll get you home."

Stopping beside me, Max whispered, "To be continued," before looking at a snoring Ivy. "Don't be too hard on her. Kids do dumb stuff."

"And you can best believe she's going to know just how dumb this shit was. I think I know how to handle my daughter."

Knowing when to back off, Max's lips grazed my cheek before he marched Toby out of my house.

I removed Ivy's shoes and covered her with a throw. Not only had she done exactly what she'd promised not to, she'd interrupted what had looked to be a spectacular night for me. The titanic hangover tomorrow was going to be the least of her problems.

SET SNITCHES REPORT TENSIONS ARE RUNNING HIGH OVER THE ADDITION OF CALYSTA JEFFRIES'S REAL-LIFE DAUGHTER, IVY. Rumor has it the stunningly gorgeous ingénue has been wowing execs with her natural talent while ruffling all sorts of bleach-blond feathers; from grande dame Alison Fairchild Roberts (Rory Lovekin) to vixen Emmy Abernathy (Gina Chiccetelli). Even sweet Shannen Lassiter (Dr. Justine Lashaway) is getting her claws out as young Ivy's current storyline sees her mysterious character, Blue Silva, snatching Pepe (Shannen's real-life amour, Javier Vásquez) out from under her perky nose! *Le scandale!* Sources say there was even a secret petition started by Jade (Jade) to have Ivy fired but co-exec producer Stanley Mercury quickly squashed it. In a recent *Soap Suds Digest* feature, Jade took a dig at the newcomer: "Ivy's kinda the weak link, no offense. She's on the soap 'cause of her mom or whatever." Hmm. Sounds like the two grapes Jade had for lunch were sour! Meanwhile, sudser audiences are anxiously awaiting the airing of Ivy Jeffries's debut episodes. Keep checking back for all the latest dish!

The Diva

CHAPTER 11

Not Even You Believe What You're Saying

Making the trek up the flowered Malibu mountain to toney Tranquility Tudor every Friday for an AA meeting was part of the bargain after crashing my car while on champagne and Xanax.

"Do you have anything new you'd like to share with the group today, Calysta?" my ex-roommate Gretchen Gibson asked as she headed the meeting.

"Not really."

Knowing by now it was pointless to push me, Gretchen moved around the room and I tuned out starlet Dolly

Burke's latest shocking share; she'd been arrested for inde-cency and a Marc Jacobs bag full of Twinkies and Skittles in a Ralphs supermarket for starters.

Sitting across from me, Erroll Cockfield, a director I'd met during my initial stay, rolled his eyes and stifled a yawn.

I tried to skip the postmeeting fireside socializing and snacks but Gretchen caught up to me, giving my arm a squeeze as she led me over to a table.

"You have to try these, Calysta, I made 'em myself," she enthused. "Besides, we haven't talked in forever, you always bolt the minute the meeting is over. I know something's bothering you, I'm very intuitive. If only people would slow down and feel their feelings. Do you have a sponsor yet?"

"No, but thanks, Gretchen, it's nothing really . . ."

"I read your daughter Ivy's on your show now," she said meaningfully. "Couldn't help but notice the cover story at the supermarket. They practically ram those things down your throat at the checkout counter. Anyway, I've been fol-lowing the story in *Soap Suds Digest*. I've started watching *R&R* since you've been back. I tell all my girlfriends I'm BFF with a soap star. They don't believe me but I don't care."

"Gretchen, I—"

Cutting me off, she continued, "Is it true them hiring your daughter has caused all kinds of tension on *The Rich and the Ruthless* set? Must be so hard for you."

"Gretchen," I interrupted as she stopped for a breath, "those stories are completely exaggerated half the time.

Having Ivy on set is a blessing. She's blending in beautifully; I'm tickled pink and so proud of her."

"Mm-hmm. Well you're better than me, Calysta, it would drive me up the wall. I love my kids, but having them at work with me twenty-four/seven? I don't think so."

"Well, we don't work together every day, Gretchen. Besides, she's one of the easiest people in the world to be around. It's great!" I forced out.

Gretchen knew better but let it slide as Dolly drifted up to us to grab a petit four. Eyes vacant, she nibbled at a corner.

"Dolly, honey?" Gretchen put an arm around her bony shoulders. "If you don't come to sobriety meetings you're not supposed to eat the snacks. It's one of the rules."

"Don't be lame, Gretch," Dolly said, grabbing two more cakes. "Mm, who needs Skittles?"

Shaking my head, I extricated myself from the duo and edged out of the room.

Soothed by the sapphire sky, I got in my Volvo and began the long winding drive home listening to my latest fave, Bishya.

Thinking about my conversation with Gretchen, I had to admit I wasn't being truthful. Things *were* tenser than ever on set and at home since Ivy had taken flight, and Stanley's fawning only fueled her bad behavior. Toby and Javier's ceaseless attention and her ramped-up storyline made Ivy's head swell to epic proportions. Her ever-growing attitude seemed unstoppable—talking trash, sparring with Jade and others, and continuing to sneak out with Toby, despite my strict orders not to. I wanted to be nothing but happy for my daughter, but if love meant drawing the line, we were at war.

* * *

Beelining it to my dressing room until I was called to set, I had no sooner glued on my lashes than Shannen pounded on my door.

"Calysta, you in there? We need to talk."

Sighing, I said, "Come in."

Quickly shutting the door behind her, looking distressed, she said, "I'm in crisis and there's no one else to tell."

"Shannen, what is it?"

"It's Ivy."

"Oh."

"You know I love her like she was . . . was, you know, like, my own sister," she said hurriedly. "She's such a beautiful, intelligent, amazing girl."

"But?"

"But I think she's trying to steal Javier from me and I just wanna punch her in her throat," she wailed, collapsing onto my sofa.

"Whoa, hold up. Shannen, that's just a storyline—"

"That's how it started for Javier and me," she argued. "I see how she looks at him, I mean, he's edible. And she's gorgeous . . . and young. You should've seen the way she touched his face to brush away crumbs—that said everything. I instantly knew there was more. I'm losing him, Calysta"—her lower lip trembled—"to Ivy!" Tears spilled.

I moved to sit beside her, patting her shoulder.

"There, there, Shannen, you're jumping to conclusions. You're not losin' Javier. Certainly not to my daughter, who's far too young for him. I'd kill him first. Plus, she's mixed up with that imbecile, Toby, sad to say."

"Is she really?" she said, sniffing. "I didn't think they were serious."

"They better not be," I said grimly. "But she's having her 'bad boy' phase and Toby fits the bill."

Shannen threw her arms around my neck. "Oh, thank you, Calysta. I'm so embarrassed dumping all my psychodrama on you. It just drives me crazy that they're writing Javier and me apart again."

"Girl, you're choking me."

"Oh, sorry." Abruptly letting go, Shannen wiped her face with her hands. "I can't believe how well you've taken it. Ivy being here and all. Can't be easy."

"Everyone keeps saying that, but I'm fine. I love having my baby on set . . . honest."

"Till now," Shannen said as she moved to my mirror to check her makeup.

"Whaddaya mean?"

"Haven't you read the new script?" she asked.

"Not yet."

"Oh . . . I should go and let you do that." She bolted from the room.

Without wasting another second, I snatched the pages, rapidly thumbing through them. It didn't take long to find the scenes Shannen was talking about.

> *Mysterious troublemaking newcomer Blue Silva rescues Ruby Stargazer from a hostage standoff at a carwash. Blue overpowers the gunman but not before Ruby takes a bullet.*
>
> *On a whim, Blue follows the wounded Ruby to the hospital where she's bleeding profusely, going into shock. Ruby needs a blood transfusion but there's a hitch—she has a rare blood type and even her daughter Jade isn't a match. On impulse Blue offers her own—a long shot. It's a match! Blue saves Ruby's life and the two share an uneasy truce before the real surprise is revealed . . . Blue Silva is Ruby Stargazer's long-lost daughter from an earlier transgression.*

Closing my eyes, I pinched the bridge of my nose with two fingers, letting the script hit the floor with a thud.

GINA

Better leave Whitehaven before you get in over
your head, Blue.

BLUE

You don't scare me, Gina. In fact, it's the other
way around.

GINA

You're bonkers, little girl.

BLUE

It's only a matter of time before I make Whitehaven and the men I desire my own.

GINA

(Sneering)

Starting with the gardener? I saw you and Pepe
in the bushes. Congratulations, you're just a
step away from bagging the butler.

BLUE

Pepe's just a stepping-stone. You should know
the drill. I have big plans, Granny, and you
ain't gonna stop me . . .

"Cut!" Emmy inappropriately shrieked. "What did you
just call me?!"

"Ivy, the granny remark has got to go," Julius said wearily.

"Thought it was a good ad-lib," Ivy said.

Watching the scene, I shook my head, half amused and half troubled.

"It was great," Stanley chimed in, stepping out of the control booth. "Loved it, the line stays."

"Are you effin' kidding me?" Emmy ranted. "This little twerp can't run around changing the lines and calling me granny."

"Excuse me, I know you're not talkin' about my daughter like that," I stepped in.

"Mom, I can take care of myself," Ivy said.

"Can we get back to taping?" Julius yelled.

"Yes, why don't you two older actresses take your cues from Ivy and behave professionally," Stanley said snidely.

For once Emmy and I were speechless at the same thing.

CHAPTER 12

Secrets of a Soap Opera Producer

Y 'low?"

"Grandma Jones, that you?"

"Who else would it be, Beulah?"

"I know, Grandma, it's just I'm . . . I'm a little inside out."

"What happ'n this time on that crazy set? Y'all need to quit it. Give yourselves a stroke with all that foolishness out there in Hollywoodland."

"It's not what you think, Grandma."

"Well what in tarnation is it? Spit it out with a quickness 'cause I don't have all day and tomorrah's not promised."

"It's Ivy."

"Don't tell me somethin's happ'n to my grandbaby."

"Somethin's happened all right, but . . ."

"C'mon, Beulah. I'm 'bout to come through the phone! I can feel my blood pressure risin' up the back of my neck."

"Ivy's got a job on *my* show."

"*The Rich and the Ruthless?*"

"Yes, ma'am."

"Well I'll be, what a blessing the two of you working together."

"Yes, a real blessing, Grandma."

"So what does she do in the office?"

"Grandma, that's what's got me worried. Ivy doesn't work in the office. She's one of the actors."

"Hold on while I catch my breath."

"Grandma, you all right?"

"All right? I'm crying out of joy, chile. First you, and now my great-grandbaby on my stories. I'm tickled. Wait till I tell Whilemina an' 'em. They're gonna just about die when they find out. Oh, yes 'n' dee-dee, we Joneses is a talented bunch." She paused. "Beulah, did you hear what I said?"

"Yes, ma'am, I heard you," I said, sniffling.

"What's wrong, you got yourself a cold? You don't sound right."

"No, I don't have a cold."

"Good, 'cause God knows I don't wanna have to come

back out d'ere knowin' that place is gonna slide right into the Pacific Ocean next earthquake."

"Grandma, I just think it's too much pressure for Ivy to be a soap star."

"*You* did it and it wasn't too much pressure for you."

"But that was different. I'm different. Ivy's had a sheltered life and isn't tough enough to deal with these haters."

"Don't you be so sure, missy. My Ivy's got a trick bag too. Why don't you give her some room to play her hand? Might be surprised. Ooo-wee, I'ma tell Eartheletta and Verline right away. Can't wait to see my Ivy on TV and on my favorite story, *The Rich and the Ruthless*. Anything else, Beulah?"

"No, ma'am, just wanted to check on you and see what you had to say about Ivy."

"Well all right then, you heard. See if I ain't right. Now you get yourself to prayin' the way I taught you to and you won't have to second-guess what God has for you or my Ivy. Be blessed, Beulah. Love you."

"Love you more, Grandma." I sadly hung up the kitchen phone as Ivy sailed in and wondered if Grandma would ever call me by my stage name, Calysta. Probably not. It was clear as day Ivy had an army of support, including our Grandma Jones.

Plucking up an Asian pear out of the fruit bowl, Ivy sang, "Hey, Mom."

"Hi, honey."

Taking a delicate bite she said, "I swear, today was cuh-ra-zy on set. Randall's losing it."

"More than usual?"

"Mm-hmm. He interrupted taping, like, ten times, switching out art and set walls, which changed our blocking, driving the director nuts."

"Sounds like a continuity thing, or . . ."

"Stanley didn't seem to think so and tore Randall a new one. He wears his executive producer badge like a sheriff."

"*Co*-executive—"

"Whatever," Ivy said, taking another bite. "Bottom line, Stanley runs the show and Randall has even less power after today's smackdown."

"Sorry I missed that."

"And you know that hot AD, right?"

"Ah, yes. I work on the show too," I said with an edge.

"He totally held it together. He's so damn cool."

"Other than Randall's craziness, how'd taping go today? I know you had big scenes with Jade and Emmy."

"Piece of cake. Stanley called me a ravishing professional. Said I knocked it out the park and exceeded expectations as a freshman. I was way better than Emmy and Jade. They totally sucked," Ivy said conceitedly, taking another microbite of her fruit before tossing it.

Before I could say a word, Ivy piped, "Gotta watch my weight."

"Baby, you don't have a thing to worry about in that department, but we do need to talk about your atti—"

"Mom, relax, those cameras add ten pounds," she said, stretching as she stood. "Jus' tryin' to protect my ass-sets," she said suggestively, patting her skinny behind.

Was that fresh conceit actually coming out of my daughter's mouth? Had I failed as a mother? I'd cry about it later.

"Mom? Mom, did you hear what I said?"

"What?"

"I said, I'm goin' out with friends later. Don't wait up," she said, ducking out of the kitchen.

I loved Ivy more than anything. I'd given her everything—maybe too much because of my own childhood—still, that was no excuse for her behavior. I'd had it easy with her till now; she'd always been a respectful girl. Her recent acting out and back talk worried me and were a sign of things to come, especially with the soap serving as a powerful influence. Everyone sewed wild oats while young, but my daughter was making it hard to stay understanding.

About to take a much-needed soak, I realized I'd forgotten my script, the one I was supposed to know by heart tomorrow, back at the set.

Retracing my steps in a robe to Ivy's room, where muffled music pulsed, I pounded on her door. She peeked out, her eyes traced with thick black eyeliner.

"Yes?"

"You have t'morrow's script?" I asked.

"Naw, already memorized my lines."

Dagger in my stomach.

"O-kay, guess I'ma have to go all the way back to set unless you . . ."

"I'll be gone by the time you get back. Drive safe. Love you." She shut the door.

* * *

The WBC studio lot at night was very *Phantom of the Opera*-ish. The night guard studied my ID for a few seconds before opening the gate.

I waved at a janitor in the hall before entering my dressing room, grabbing my script from the sofa.

"Calysta?" said a voice behind me.

Jumping out of my skin, I saw Ben standing in my doorway, awkwardly holding a large painting in his arms.

"Jeezus, Ben! You scared me."

"Sorry, I was heading down to the set and saw your door open."

"Forgot my script. What are you doing here so late?"

"Putting a last-minute touch on tomorrow's set."

"Shouldn't the crew be doing that?"

Ben looked at me nervously. "I'm just doing what Randall told me to do. I don't ask questions." He disappeared down the hall.

What was Randall was up to now? One thing was for sure: it couldn't be good.

CHAPTER 13

Top Frog

At his McMansion, a disgruntled Phillip McQueen stormed down to the basement.

"PINKEY!" he yelled over his shoulder. "Bring tomorrow's script and don't forget the mustache!"

"Coming, Phillip," his wife replied, balancing his tea and with her knitting tucked under one arm.

Phillip had converted the basement into a replica of the *Rich and the Ruthless* set for rehearsing demanding scenes without the irritation of Wolfe, Calysta, and others. It included a duplicate life-sized portrait of himself as his character, Barrett Fink.

"There's a Sudsy in this scene, but it's with that saboteurial blowhard, Wolfe."

"Phillip, dear, I think he pronounces it 'Volfe.' "

"Pinkey! Who cares? The man can't even say his own pathetic name! Drives me crazy he doesn't have a W in his vocabulary. That foreigner will try anything to distract me, like twisting the ends of his musty mustache or some upstagery like that. It's imperative that I know every syllable, Wolfe's lines as well as mine; that I refine my delivery to its highest mantle so that my mesmerizing performance will scream Sudsy Award!" he cried, one fist thrust toward the speckled basement ceiling.

"Yes, darling," Pinkey soothed, thrilled to help, slapping on a mock mustache. Rehearsing lines with her husband was Pinkey's taste of life outside of PTA meetings, Walmart, and being a housewife. She cherished each and every moment.

Taking a sip of tea, Phillip positioned himself; an electric fireplace aglow, one hand resting on the back of a wingback chair, he turned his haughty face to profile.

"I'm ready."

Pinkey held the pages at arm's length, adjusting her reading glasses. Clearing her throat, she channeled the Wolfe character and applied a very bad European accent.

VIDAL

You von't get away vith this, you vermin.

BARRETT

And what do you think you can possibly do, old man?

VIDAL

I vill destroy you, Fink, and make you pay if it's the last thing I do.

Breaking character, Pinkey exclaimed, "Oh, Phillip, it sounds so exciting!"

"Pinkey!" Phillip thundered. "You broke the fourth wall and killed my momentum."

"I'm s-sorry, b-but that was the end of the scene."

"The end? Impossible."

Pinkey fumbled with the pages. "Vidal's line is the tag and then it goes to Pepe."

"Let me see that," he snapped, snatching the script, moistening the tip of his index finger. "Where's my monologue! Un-friggin'-believable, my raison d'être is to *act* and I'm thwarted at every turn. I'm too good for this show. Bastards! Veronica gives Wolfe my tagline . . ."

"Phillip dear, let me get your tea."

". . . then cuts to Spanglish pretty boy Javier with Calysta's brat, Ivy, giving these circus actors more lines? I can't take it anymore, Pinkey . . . what's the point of going on?"

"Because you're a professional, Phillip," Pinkey delivered like a 1940s film star.

"That goes without saying. But I won't be winning any Sudsy for this drivel. Javier or that Ivy Jeffries will. Fucked-up childhoods always walk away with the awards."

"Phillip!"

"I'm sorry, Pinkey, but why did I have to grow up with a happy family?" he lamented, heading to the couple's frilly bedroom, bordering on a whorehouse boudoir.

"I don't know, dear," answered Pinkey, following.

Dabbing eye caviar, his nightly preening ritual, Phillip continued with splintering anger. "That Mexican, Javier, actually said he was 'bred to be epic,' can you believe it? Then he attacked me with a bunch of Spanish babble. When I demanded a translation he said, 'Where you're go-een I already wee-nt, sat down, had a soda and came back.' Probably some kind of Latino gang threat."

"*Donde tu vas, yo ya fui, me senté, me tomé una soda, y regresé,*" Pinkey recited.

"What?" asked an astonished Phillip.

"Judge Milian says it on *The People's Court* all the time," Pinkey said proudly, starting to knit. "It's my favorite. I watch it every day, even the reruns."

"Pinkey! Where's your support? My reputation is hanging in the balance, constantly threatened by insipid producers and overacting fools I'm forced to work with. Why can't anyone see that Javier and Ivy shouldn't even be on the show?"

Putting on the final touches of the third eye cream under both baby blues, he cried, "It's unspeakable torture, all my Meisner training wasted. How could Javier have two shows, three endorsements, make millions with no acting training? I'm calling Augustus to tell him if he doesn't give me what I want, I'm walking."

"But, Phillip, with the recession . . ."

"Fuck the recession!"

"Phillip!" Pinkey exclaimed, binding off the back of another sweater for the *Rich and the Ruthless* fan club luncheon.

"No, Pinkey, I'm mad as hell," Phillip spat, punching his pillow before kicking off his *R&R* slippers, getting into bed. "I am daytime drama and I can't wimp out. Not now. If I get eclipsed by those kids, *R&R* will lose their audience, their number one status, and worse than that, go to a half hour. And if that happens they might as well sunset the show and pull the plug. I wouldn't be caught dead doing a half hour of anything."

"But, dear, what about our time-share on Oahu and Bert's astronaut camp in Cape Canaveral?"

"We'll be fine," Phillip said, popping an Ambien. "*The Rich and the Ruthless* isn't going to a half hour any more than Javier's getting nominated for a Sudsy Award," he assured, pulling his toile blindfold over his eyes.

Clearing her throat, putting her size 10 knitting needles down, Pinkey suggestively said, "Phillip, honey, I know you said you'd never do a half hour of anything, and I know it's not calendared, but do you think we could . . ."

"Pinkey, like you said, I'm a professional. I've got a big day on set tomorrow. It's like being a boxer: I can't waste my strength on frivolity if I expect to win!" He rolled over and was out like a light.

Disappointed again, a sexually deprived Pinkey put her knitting away and flipped open her laptop, clicking on her favorite soft-core erotica website to order more products.

CHAPTER 14

Warning Signs

BLUE

It's true, Ruby, I'm your long lost-daughter. The blood test from the hospital proves it.

RUBY

My daughter! I knew you'd find me. Please forgive me but I had to put you up for adoption. I was young, homeless, and illiterate. You're so beautiful!

BLUE

Thanks.

JADE

Wait, Mom, how do we know Blue is who she says she is? I'm supposed to accept her as my half sister just like that? I don't think so.

RUBY

Jade, darling, I won't love you any less. I believe Blue. It's so important to me that you do too. All I want is for us to be one happy family.

JADE

But, Mom, she's a fraud . . . I can feel it! She's only after your money . . . she's an interscoper . . .

"Cut!" Julius barked.

"Why? What happened?" Jade asked.

"The word is *interloper*," Ivy corrected snottily.

" 'Scuse you," Jade retorted. "I've been on *R&R*, like, five years longer than you."

"We'd never know," shot Ivy.

"That's enough," I intervened.

"Yeah, like, listen to your *mommy*," Jade teased.

Flushing, Ivy said, "I got this . . . Calysta."

I couldn't believe my ears. *"Whadid you say?"*

"Okay, ladies," Julius interrupted. "How 'bout we save the family drama for the camera? Pick it up from Jade's last line."

"That's five," the stage manager called.

"Sonofa—" Julius cursed.

Pulling Ivy to the side, I whispered furiously, "Have you gone and lost your natural mind talking to me like that, calling me Calysta?"

Scowl-faced, Ivy said, "Same difference as you talking to me like a child while I'm trying to work. We're not at home; treat me like an equal, with respect."

"I will when you prove you deserve it and get some sense, not like a conceited brat," I said, voice rising. "Nevah woulda let you do this gig if I knew it was gonna blow your head up like this."

"Let me? I'm eighteen, in case you forgot, and you have no say."

"As long as you're livin' in my house and I'm payin' the bills I'd say I have ALL the say. Now if you don't lose the nasty attitude, see if I don't look good slappin' that fresh right outta ya."

"What the hell is going on here?" Stanley said, intruding. "Do I need to call security, Ivy?"

"No, Stanley. Mom and I were just havin' a little misunderstanding."

"Calysta, you're disturbing the entire set, threatening Ivy. I don't take that lightly considering your history of violence."

Noticing most of the cast had gathered to gawk, I wondered if this was Stanley's plan all along. Probably.

He no doubt was itchin' to call security, that prick. I'd be damned if I was going to give him the satisfaction.

"We cool, Ivy?"

My daughter's eyes darted from me to Stanley and back. "Um. Yeah."

Looking disappointed, he nodded. "Good. Glad that's resolved. But consider this your first strike, Calysta. C'mon, Ivy, let's get some lunch, my treat. Wanna talk to you about your next cover shoot." They trotted off arm in arm.

"If that was my kid, I woulda knocked that brat on her keester," Maeve grumbled, shuffling up behind me, stinking of nicotine. "Spare the rod, spoil the child."

"I'm not gonna beat my daughter, Maeve."

Fed up, I decided enough was enough and too much was foolish.

* * *

Randall was engrossed in an *ART PAPERS* magazine and didn't look up as I stepped into his shoe box office.

"Have a minute, Randall?"

"Not for you," he muttered.

"Now that's not nice. And no way to talk to a lady who

you have so much history with," I said pointedly, shutting the door to give us privacy.

"What are you yammering about now, Calysta? I'm busy."

"And you're about to be even busier helping me with this Stanley/Ivy business."

Slamming down the magazine, Randall looked up, asking, "Why would I help you?"

"Because you hate Stanley more than I do."

"So."

"So I don't tell Veronica you're being uncooperative."

"You're in no position to threaten me, Calysta . . . I mean, Beulah. Don't forget our little secret about your daddy in Mississippi."

"You tried to bully me with that mess once before, it's not happenin' again." Taking a gamble, I added with a poker face, "And you're having Ben run around the set after hours hanging paintings *for* . . ."

Blood draining from his panicked face, Randall took the bait, snapping, "You don't know what you're talking about, but if it means you keeping your mouth shut, I'll help if I can. You're crazy if you think I have any power over Mercury though."

"Don't play me, you go to sleep and wake up thinking of ways to bump off that jackass. You know Stanley and Edith's angle bringing my daughter on *R&R*?"

Randall nodded yes.

"Start singing," I ordered.

Satisfied fifteen minutes later, I left his stifling office, almost colliding with Max.

"What are you doin' up here?" I asked.

"They got me doing three jobs. How 'bout you, everything okay?" He was looking curiously at Randall's door.

"Yep."

Taking one of my hands, he said, "You know, you should call me sometime."

"I'll keep that in mind," I said, and kept it movin'.

"Why do I feel like you're keeping something from me, Calysta?"

Over one shoulder, I said, "We all keep things from each other, Max. Aren't you guilty?"

TALK ABOUT TWO TICKETS TO TROUBLE IN PARADISE.
Word is *Rich and the Ruthless*'s demoted producer Randall
Roberts and his sartorially challenged diva wife, Alison Fair-
child Roberts (Rory Lovekin, *R&R*), have been experiencing
a marital meltdown and may be heading for the big D—and
I don't mean "daytime." Set spies say Randall is looking
mighty cozy with scheming siren Emmy Abernathy (Gina
Chiccetelli, *R&R*). And that's just the tip of the "on-set ro-
mance" iceberg. *Quel scandale!* You know what they say:
"Love in the afternoon is a minefield."

The Diva

CHAPTER 15

What a Tangled Web We Weave

A lison, are you up there?" Randall yelled from the foyer of their mansion.

"Yeah!" she screamed, "in my Barbie room," stuffing a chunk of dusted chocolate in her mouth.

Stepping off the mirrored elevator, Randall headed down the hall on the fourth level and entered her creepy space as she hung up her Princess phone, licking her fingers.

"Who were you talking to?" Randall inquired.

"Nobody," Alison dismissed, brushing a Pilgrim Barbie's hair.

"And do we have to talk in here?" he asked with claustropho-

bic disgust, gazing at *Diamond Dazzle Barbie, Princess of Ancient Mexico Barbie,* and hundreds more covering every surface in the room along with Barbie's friends, pool house, car, and accessories.

"Yes, we do. It's soothing to be with my dolls."

"Better be important for you to call me off set in the middle of the day. You know this is a strategic time for me, can't be seen slacking off."

"Don't you mean it's a strategic time for us?" Alison said dangerously, trading out half a truffle for another.

"What?"

Swallowing then running her tongue over her teeth, she bit, "It's a strategic time for us. You keep leaving me out of the loop. I don't appreciate it."

"Are you mad?" an agitated Randall said. "You called me away from . . ."

". . . your important work in that shared broom closet of an office? Or did I interrupt another forged art deal using R&R as an 'in plain sight' black market auction house, padding your fatass pockets behind my back!"

Instantly sweating, Randall began, "How—"

"Calysta told me!" Alison shrieked, choking the lifeless doll. "Here I've been slaving to make ends meet after your sorry ass landed in the hospital; fired my chef, my trainer, and cut out hydrocolonic therapy completely. And all along you've been friggin' cheatin' me out of my share? You bastard!"

"Alison, my Mona Lisa . . ."

"Don't 'Mona Lisa' me!"

"I did it for us," Randall pleaded. "I was going to surprise you. Besides, if anything went south, I didn't want you implicated."

"You're fullashit." Winging Pilgrim Barbie at him, Alison bolted down the hall, off the elevator, and into their master bedroom—the ceiling frescoed with angels and sonnets, every stick of furniture drunk with gold leaf. The furious daytime diva viciously tore Randall's clothes from hangers, throwing them over the terrace balcony and into the pool.

"For crissakes," Randall cried, charging into the room. "Stop, Alison, you're overreacting!"

"Am I?" she stormed, chocolate caked in the corners of her mouth giving her a Joker appearance.

"I made a terrible mistake not telling you," Randall pleaded.

"Did you ever. This ain't about another sleazy potluck affair like with that hobag, Emmy. This is real betrayal! Now, get out!"

"We can get past this, sugarplum. I'll make it up to you, my queen . . ."

"Get out!" she screamed.

But before Randall could escape Alison's wrath she launched an armful of Guccis and spat, "I want a divorce!"

*   *   *

Randall's *R&R* office door slammed shut, startling him upright in his chair, heart pounding, rubbing phantom pain all over his head from the nightmare. Emmy stood in front of his desk, wrapped in an Emanuel Ungaro mini, with stilettos, postsex hair, and red nails.

"Emmy? What is it?" a shaken Randall asked.

"Read about all the drama with Alison. Why didn't you come to Mamma, tell me all about it? Just had to check on my poor snuggle bunny," Emmy purred, pouring herself onto his lap. "You okay?"

"Oh, Emmy, my life's in shambles," Randall cried. "I don't know what to . . ."

Emmy interrupted, forcing a sloppy wet one, tickling his love handles.

Eagerly kissing her back before breaking away, he half-heartedly protested, "Emmy, I can't do this again, remember—"

As she guided his hand under her skirt, the vixen said, "You don't need that trollop you call your wife, Randy. She's totally holding you back." Emmy could sense weakness like a shark smells blood. She stroked Randall's flabby chest and ego with one hand, unzipping his pants with the other. She pressed her scarlet lips to his ear.

"Think what we could do together."

Randall moaned as Emmy's hand skillfully fiddled inside his Brooks Brothers.

"You haven't been able to hot-wire control of *R&R,* but with my help, you could own this show and everyone on it."

CHAPTER 16

Love in the Afternoon
(Is a Minefield)

*D*oor ajar, I crossed the threshold into the suite. After I vented to Max for days about Ivy and my insufferable job, he suggested I take a load off and meet him at the Beverly Hills Hotel. My call. Said he'd be there rain or shine and promised to help me forget my superstresses.

Making my way to the French doors, biting my lower lip in anticipation, I kicked off the Manolos and sank deeper into the thick carpeting, reminded of running barefoot in the sensuous Mississippi moss. Only thing missing from this scene was a soap opera fan blowing my weave in slow mo. Oh well, good thing I'd slipped a pair of MojoNights in my purse. I sensed I was in for something special.

Warpaint's "Don't You Call Anybody Else Baby" played louder as I opened the doors, taking in the sumptuous bedroom aglow with flickering honeysuckle candles.

"Oh wow . . ."

Not wasting any time, Max, GQ handsome in jeans and shirtless, headed toward me with two glasses of champagne.

I liked his speed and his style.

"Tryin' to seduce me, Mr. Gardner?"

"Absolutely," he replied, raising his glass. "To us."

I kissed my glass to his, faking a sip. Didn't feel like telling my life story.

"Hungry?" he asked.

"Mmm, not for food," I flirted.

Max set our glasses down before softly tracing the curve of my neck with his fingertips, dropping a smoldering kiss on my lips. Aching to trust the connection and lay my troubles down for the night, it was all the invitation I needed to lean my body against his, deepening the embrace.

Strong arms encircling me, heat radiated off his spicy chest as he effortlessly swept me up and carried me to the pillowed bed, where we melted into the luxurious comforter, fit for a Turkish sultan. Passion in every touch, our lips hungrily searching, pawing at each other's clothes.

Gently stripping me down to my sultry Kiki de Montparnasse lingerie, Max groaned, "You're so damn delicious."

"Ditto."

Removing my lacy thong, he lowered his chiseled face, amorously tracing kisses across my breasts and every pulse point. Under a shimmering moon, our bodies recklessly fell into wet, animalistic thunder-and-lightning sex. As my fingers combed his hair, Max moved back up to meet my mouth. Trading dirty nothings, he parted my moist thighs with one of his. Wrapping my legs around him tightly, I drew him in deeper.

Jeweled with each other's perspiration, love was definitely on lockdown as adrenaline soared higher, higher, and higher still. Pickin' up the pace, on the verge of climax, I screamed, "DON'T STOP! DONFUCKINGSTOP! Don'uggin'op . . . 'ere I come, 'ere I come, 'ere . . . I . . . COMMMMMMMME!"

Arching in ecstasy, molten lava bursting again, and again, and yes, again. An exhausted Max exhaled, "Fuckin' awesome," before collapsing.

He had done most of the work after all. Still, I was always amazed how men could instantly slide into a snorefest after lovemaking. Me? I was wide awake, extraordinarily blissful and renewed. Ready to do a marathon.

Experiencing a spark I hadn't felt in a long time, I was scared to be so hopeful about someone I'd only just met. I tried to swallow my fear as I got up and expertly reapplied my makeup, now regretting I didn't cap it with a MojoNight.

"Calysta?"

"I'm still here," I said, reappearing soap opera perfect, climbing back into bed to straddle Max.

Plucking up a huge strawberry from the bowl on the nightstand, I held it between my teeth and leaned forward, quenching both our thirsts by sharing fruit. Nectar burst on our tongues, juice dripping on the sheets.

"If only things could stay this sweet," I nakedly confessed.

A smile tugged at Max's mouth as he tenderly cupped my face, assuring, "Don't worry, I'm not gonna let you get away, and you know what else?"

"What?" I asked as he pulled me down beside him.

"I always get what I go after."

CHAPTER 17

Dog Days

Still basking in the afterglow of my fabulous endorphin-releasing night with Max, I breezed through the next day on my own personal cloud nine, unruffled by Phillip's antics or being cornered by one of Maeve's "good ole days blues club" stories. Amused, I spied Max listening with rapt attention to the wrinkled soap star, interrupting, "Really somethin', isn't it, Max?"

"Almost like being there. She's quite the storyteller."

"Isn't she? Maeve, why don't you tell Max one of your Edgar Cayce accounts? Or better yet, when you were a nun in Missouri."

"A nun?" Though desperate to get away, Max couldn't resist knowing more.

"Well, let me tell you . . ." Maeve began as I slipped past, heading for my dressing room.

"What's gotten into you, Calysta?" Shannen asked, out of breath.

"Whaddaya mean?"

"I called your name a half dozen times. Seems like your head's somewhere else. You're grinning ear to ear. Only one thing can cause . . . Wait, did you get . . ." Shannen tried to ask.

"What? No," I protested. Was it that obvious?

"You're sure wearin' that 'I got me some last night' smile. I totally have radar about these things and you look oh-so-sat-is-fied," she declared.

Taking in her wide eyes, I laughed, shaking my head. "Girl, you have some imagination. If I decide to go down that crazy road again you'll be the first to know."

Shannen shrugged and skedaddled.

Aside from knowing dipping the pen in company ink was never a good idea, why didn't I trust sharing my secret about Max with Shannen? Just couldn't risk her telling Javier. Ivy might blab, but thanks to her self-involvement she was clueless Max and I had been seeing each other. Naw, my instincts were right. I'd best keep my affair under wraps—for now.

* * *

"Calysta, Emmy, Ethan, Ivy, five minutes, scene forty, be camera ready," the stage manager announced.

"Hey, beautiful, thanks for leaving me hostage with Maeve," Max said sotto voce as I passed him on my way to set. "She can talk for ten minutes straight without taking a breath."

"Who you tellin'?" I shot back. "Impressive considering she smokes like a chimney and only has one lung."

Giving my arm a squeeze, he asked, "Seven o'clock?"

"Sure, but let's keep this—"

"Not a word."

Noticing Ivy walking toward us, I added loudly, "Okay, thanks for the script changes."

"No problem," Max said, confused until Ivy brushed by with a classic teenage "my mom is so weird" look.

I turned to follow her, my cloud nine temporarily rained on.

Arriving on set, she flopped onto the Stargazer apartment chaise and whipped out a nail file, studiously ignoring me. Thinking turnabout was fair play, I returned the favor, letting my thoughts drift back to mouthwatering Max and our date tonight. He was keepin' the location a secret again and that was just fine with me. I loved having a take-charge man, having the least amount of responsibility for a change.

Emmy sauntered onto set with a yapping puff of white fur tucked firmly in the crook of her arm.

"Emmy, for the thousandth time, you can't bring your dog on set. It's against company policy, it's disruptive, and—" This from Julius.

"Relax, Jules, rules are for the newbies," she remarked, wedging the writhing pooch more firmly under her armpit.

"Who you screw doesn't make you important," Ivy muttered without looking up.

"Listen, you little . . ." Emmy started, her pooch growling. "Bad Bootsie!" she scolded, dumping her on the floor where she tugged frantically at her rhinestone leash.

"Another dog, Emmy?" Ethan asked as he finished tying his tie. "That's not your Pomapoo, is it?"

"Thanks for noticing, Ethan," she sniffed. "It's really difficult to talk about, but Pom Pom is no longer . . . no longer with me."

"Bummer, how'd she die?" Ethan asked sympathetically.

"She didn't," Emmy huffed. "Well, probably not. The shelter said she had a week to get readopted. Had to let her go. She kept peeing on my brand-new carpeting."

"Double bummer," Ethan said, picking out his Kid 'n Play.

"Yeah, double bummer," Julius blandly repeated.

"By the way, did anyone notice my new gold BMW convertible with matching rims?"

"Yeah, nice wheels, Emmy," Ethan pandered.

"It's a gift! At first it was really, really, really hard for me to let go of Pom Pom, but the car really, really, really helped a lot. I found the courage to get over it. After all, she was only a dog."

Silence.

"Touching, but you still can't have your dog on set," Julius tried again.

"My VIP doggie trainer says Bootsie needs to be by my side at all times to know I'm her mommy," Emmy protested. "Just look at her, isn't she precious? She's a Bolognese. They were the favorites of nobility and ladies-in-waiting, ya know."

"What's on her teeth?" Ethan asked as her pet growled at him.

"Doggie braces! She needed a little work to be up to snuff. I'm gonna show her at one of those Madison Square Garden dog competitions. Took her to the best pet orthodontist in Hollywood, and when I get done with her she'll be perfect."

"Are we seriously havin' this discussion?" I butt in.

"Typical hard-hearted Calysta." Emmy pouted, yanking on Bootsie's leash after she'd peed on a camera base.

"What's the holdup?" Stanley demanded, striding onto set with Randall and Alison trailing. "And what the devil is that mop doing on stage? This isn't Animal Planet."

"Randy, help, they're being so mean to me and Bootsie," Emmy whimpered.

"Randy?" Alison mouthed suspiciously, giving him a dangerous look.

A flustered Randall tried to appease both women, saying, "Everyone, please have a little compassion for Emmy, you know her pets are her family."

"Yeah, right. Family she sheds like snakeskin every time she buys a new toy," Ivy muttered.

"Randall, you know the no-pet policy as well as the rest of us," barked Stanley.

"Yeah, the damn bitch just peed on my camera," a salty cameraman added.

"Plain nasty, like some people," snarled Alison.

Emmy's eyes saucered as Randall ordered, "Ben, take Bootsie to Emmy's dressing room," snapping his fingers.

"Sure—animal wrangler, that's in my job description," Ben muttered.

"Emmy, don't let this happen again," Randall warned, earning him a glare from his lover. He wheeled back to the control booth and I hit my mark.

GINA

Shoulda known Blue was your spawn, Ruby. She's a

mirror image—a manipulative, straight-up bitch!

(Stepping in closer, raising her

hand to strike Blue)

RUBY

(Slides between Gina and Blue)

Lay a hand on my girl and I'll knock you silly.

GINA

Geez, Ruby, *you people* are always so violent—

"Cut," Julius yelled before I could. "Emmy, stop with the improv."

"Sure can dish it out, Calysta, but y'can't take it," Emmy protested.

"Jus' lay off the 'you people' stuff," I warned.

"I meant 'you people' as in the Stargazers."

Bootlickin' Ethan chimed in, "I totally got that, Emmy."

"Good grief, Calysta, you're like one of those civil rights extremists," Emmy spat. "Always hurling yourself on a pyre or beating your breasts over nothin'. I have news for you: We got you off this show once and it was your own damn fault. We can do it again."

"We?" I asked.

"Yeah, the network and . . ."

"Emmy, that's enough," a red-faced Randall reemerged from the control booth. "Eighty-six the comments and stick to the script," he emphasized.

Another public smackdown. I absolutely enjoyed taking in Emmy's cracked face. In fact, the whole crew did.

After a long, tense moment, Emmy wordlessly turned on her heels and stalked off the set.

* * *

"Girl, you shoulda been there, Randall dissed Emmy good; bet she still got that bitter aftertaste in her big trap," I gossiped to one of my oldest girlfriends, Zylissa.

"Damn. Not ta squash your story, but I was callin' 'cause I got news of my own."

"What's that?" I asked.

"'Member when I was all busted, 'bout to get evicted, no money, no nothin', catchin' a bus to get from A to B?"

"Yeah . . ."

"Well, I got sick and tired of bein' sick and tired of waitin' for a gig. Knowing full well I coulda pee'd all over a role if only one existed."

"Yeah, get to the point?"

"Well, 'member I was thinkin' of findin' me a sugar daddy, even if he was old as dirt?"

"C'mon, Zylissa, this ain't the box set of *Girls Gone Wild*, out with it," I said impatiently.

"'Member how them casting directors were drivin' me crazy, always goin' for *light skin, long hair*?"

"Mm-hmm."

"Well, I cut off my dreads and dyed my micro'fro and brows platinum!"

"You *what?*"

"You heard me."

"And I told you to keep your hair the way it was, it was beautiful . . . it was you! Damn shame you let Hollywood rob you from you. Now you're gonna look like everybody else—well not quite."

"Lemme finish, Calysta."

"Go 'head."

" 'Member how I was stressin' 'bout gettin' that Valtrex commercial and . . ."

"You booked it . . ." I interrupted, desperate for my friend to get to the meat.

"Well, a producer saw it and hired me as the lead on a new web series!"

"Hallelujah!" I exclaimed, half out of joy for Zylissa and half because we were about to hang up. "Have you started workin' yet?"

"Uh-huh, wanted to get an episode in the can 'fore I called 'cause you know how these shady fools be. Cancel your ass off a show in a heartbeat over the shape of your nose."

"Ain't that the truth. But tell me, what's the name of your web series?" I asked.

"Okay, first of all, like I said it's on the web, not network."

"Girl, gig's a gig, jus' tell me."

"It's called *The Furious Lives of Fly Girls and Buttermilk Lesbians,*" she said proudly.

"Wow, Zy," I managed after a moment, trying not to sound judgmental. "Sounds really entertainin'."

"Yep. Already got an interview on BuzzWorthy radio and might be goin' on *Family Feud* for an antibullying charity. Love Steve Harvey. He's part of my inspiration. Look at the success he's had since cuttin' off all his hair."

"Right. Sounds like you got a lot goin' on," I said, amazed, weighing in on what a little trashy TV bought these days.

"You wanna come visit me on set?"

"Um, yeah, 'course, but why don't you get a few episodes under your belt first and I'll pop by."

"Cool beans, can't wait for you to meet the cast."

"Definitely," I replied, unsure what I was getting myself into. "But seriously, Zylissa, I'm happy for you."

"Yeah, it only took five years to get a friggin' J-O-B in Hollywood, but I got me one now. They don't know it yet, but they won't be able to shake me with a stick."

"Zylissa, do yourself a favor and know you don't have to do whatever they ask you to do on camera," I warned.

"Whaddaya mean? Like Jennifer Beals and 'em on *The L Word* or Victoria Rowell on *Noah's Arc*?" Zylissa sucked her teeth and stated matter-of-factly, "Shoot, I'ma do whatever they tell me with a smile and take it all the way to the bank. I'm tired of fightin' and bein' broke, Calysta. Don't even know what or who I'm fightin' for anymore. Everyone's been bought off. Tell me I'm wrong, I'll call you a liar."

We hung up. My heart sank. I knew Zylissa wasn't

wrong. Her heroes were Nina Simone, bell hooks, and Angela Davis. Seemed she'd traded down to Kim Kardashian,
Snooki, and *America's Got Talent*. But who was I to judge her?
Zylissa was right. Where was the leadership? What the hell
happened?

*   *   *

"What the hell was that?" Emmy fumed, stomping into
Randall's office, lodging herself in front of his desk, planting
fists on her bony hips.

Steeling himself, he calmly raised a placating hand.
"Now, snookums . . ."

"Shut up, shithead. You embarrassed me in front of the
entire cast and crew, I've never been so humiliated in my *life*.
Why were you sticking up for that bitch, Calysta, anyway?"

"Emmy, you're upset," Randall said carefully, knowing he was skating on thin ice and not wanting to see what
would happen if it cracked. "How 'bout you open a split of
bubbles in my minifridge and cool off."

Uncrossing her scrawny arms, planting her red acrylics
on Randall's desk, Emmy dangerously leaned in like a pan-
ther, whispering, "I ain't thirsty," through clenched teeth.

"I'm sorry I hurt you," a conciliatory Randall said, mask-
ing his angst, launching into a well-rehearsed excuse. "Veronica needs to see me playing nice with teacher's pet. It'll
shine a good light on me and increase my chances of boot-
ing Stanley out of my seat."

"That still doesn't justify the way you talked to me on set," Emmy insisted, stamping her foot. "Do whatcha hafta do to win, but don't ever do it at my expense ever again! And I ain't kissin' Calysta's ass, no matter what the incentive. Got it?"

"Emmy, my pet"—he backpedaled—"I wasn't clear. What I meant to say was you're oceans better than she is. Be the bigger person, ignore Calysta's ghetto behavior."

"Should've fired her when you had the chance, not negotiating with her now!"

"Baby, I can't fire anyone till I'm back in control. But when that happens, I guarantee Calysta and her bastard brat, Ivy, will feel the tip of my boot so far up their asses . . . I'll make sure it sticks this time."

"Fine . . . I guess. And for crissakes tell the soap rags if they don't lay off reporting my birthday you're gonna take away on-set visiting privileges or somethin' threatenin' like that. How am I supposed to play ingénue when those creeps keep printing my real friggin' age?"

Relieved he'd survived a potential maelstrom, circling from around his desk, Randall soothed, "Shhh, my little masterpiece. I'll take care of it."

"You betta', Daddy," Emmy said, pouting.

Wrapping his flabby arms around Emmy's 0 waist, he instructed, "Now reach into Pappie's pockets and make him smile."

CHAPTER 18

Undercover Shocker

The next day, I walked across the WBC parking lot with a spring in my step. Not even Ivy storming out of the house this morning after a stupid argument was dampening my spirits after last night's interlude with Max. Couldn't stop thinking about him.

Passing Stanley Mercury's boat of a car, I noticed a large, black A strategically taped along his license plate, turning BOSS into ASS. Giggling inside, I continued into the studio.

Nearly run over by Randall being chased by Max, I peeled myself from the wall and joined others hightailing it to set to find Max snappin' cuffs on a winded, sweaty, red-faced Randall, yanking him roughly to his feet.

"We'll be outta here shortly. I'm Detective Gardner, LAPD."

"Is this some sort of joke?" fumed Alison.

"'Fraid not," Max replied as two uniformed officers flanked her husband.

Shock filled the set as Alison spat nails, saying, "Hey, listen, you wannabe director . . ."

"Actually, I'm a detective, Detective Gardner." Redirecting his attention, he recited, "Randall Roberts, you're under arrest. You have the right to remain silent . . ."

I couldn't believe what I was seeing or hearing. Max, or whatever his real name was, played me to get to Randall? How could I be so gullible? So desperate for love? Max was just another trapdoor.

As the cops marched a humiliated Randall off the *Rich and the Ruthless* stage past cast and crew, Max stopped in front of me and I tried like hell to hold back my tears.

His eyes attempting to soften the sadness in mine, he gently said, "It was all necessary. Sorry, Calysta," before pushing through the heavy padded door.

* * *

Hungry soap press quickly clung to the news like flies to . . . well, you know. Everywhere I turned cast mates were embellishing their accounts of the events—though no one knew the full story—most turning the impromptu interview into a showcase for themselves.

Cliffhanger Weekly reporter Mitch Morelli attempted to get a statement out of Veronica Barringer.

"Given the tenuous climate in daytime and after today's bruising allegations of fraud and forgery on the *Rich and the Ruthless* set, are you worried about the potential blowback this could cause?" he asked the soap opera heiress.

"Mitch, *R&R*'s reputation does not fall on one person's shoulders, or their unscrupulous mistakes. There's plenty of sunshine on the horizon," she responded smoothly. "That's all I have to say on the matter for now. If you'll excuse me."

Narrow popularity never dissuaded Phillip from swooping in for face time with the press. As he yammered on about being an indispensable accessory to the soap, Wolfe Hudson sidled up next to me, decked in Christian Dior, casually observing, "Look at all these idiots running around like farm ants on Prozac."

"Hmmm . . ."

Taking an elegant drag from a Dunhill, he recited, " 'Hell is other people.' Sartre."

"Sounds about right," I responded.

With an uneasy truce on set and deadlock silence at home, things couldn't have been more tense between Ivy and me, but to my surprise, at that very moment she slipped her hand into mine and said, "I'm sorry, Mom . . . about Max."

Had to ask myself why hadn't I tried to mend the fence first with my daughter—why was I so damn stubborn?

"Gonna be okay?" she asked.

"Of course," I said with love. "All that matters is that *we're* okay."

Emmy's ceaseless blah-blahing could be heard across the set as she used Randall's misfortune to go self-servingly off topic, as usual.

"I'm s'ho-ho upset," Emmy stuttered to Mitch. "Stress makes me break out in neck h-h-hives like Chelsea Lately. Plus, I'm trying to start a family!"

"Really? You're pregnant?"

"Gawd no!" Emmy said, miraculously finding her composure. "Ruin my skin? Wouldn't be caught dead with stretch marks. My beauty's my bread and butter. I'm adopting . . . from Africa."

"Right, you keep talking about that."

"Maybe a Somalian kid. Can't be bothered with the braids 'n' kink thing. Not that I have anything against kink." She grinned. "It just looks like *so* much trouble. I'm a working actor, who has time? Besides, if I had a kid with hair problems like Calysta's, what would I do? Between the pressing, the perming, those crazy hot combs . . . I'd go nuts."

"Emmy, how did we get so off topic?" Mitch nudged. "We were talking about Randall's arrest. Speaking of stress, I imagine Alison's pretty stressed herself right now."

"That's what she gets for marrying a criminal," Emmy

said heartlessly. "Aren't you going to ask about the Nymph Awards? I'm nominated!"

"Actually—" Mitch started but Emmy barreled on.

"Love the French. They know how to do cheese, grapes, fancy lingerie, and good-lookin' guys. Ooh la la, can't beat Monte Carlo in the summer. Everyone's out there naked bakin' their buns on the beach building sandcastles to the sky. I'm, like, the only American allowed where Prince Albert sunbathes. I was so honored when the prince asked me to put some of my Coppertone on his backside. Just know I'm gonna win the Nymph this year."

As Ivy and I made our way through the crush of parading bodies we passed a red-eyed Alison, with a ridiculous *I Dream of Jeannie* ponytail perched on and pinned to the crown of her head, crying to another soap reporter.

"Omigod, this is the worst disaster that's ever happened to me! I'm devastated. I had no idea my husband, Randall, was involved in anything illegal," she sobbed, pointedly adding, "I'd like that on record. But I could *feel* the dishonesty in our marriage, it was tearing me apart. If only I'd accepted that *Damages* contract, but that man-faced Glenn Close snatched it right out from under me. I'd be light-years away from this madness."

"I don't know what to say, Alison. But thanks for the . . ."

"While I have you here, I'd like to send a message of bubbles and kisses to all my adoring fans. . . ."

"Okay."

Grabbing the tape recorder, Alison shut her eyes and monologued, "Thank you, my dear, dear, dearest fans, for helping me pluck up the courage to have my breast-reduction surgery. As you know, I've had a lot of problems—most recently one of them malfunctioned and I had to be rushed to the hospital from the *R&R* set. Thank you for all the get-well musical cards, Barbie balloons, and carnations. I was in surgery for hours, and if you want to live my experience I put the pictures up on YouTube. They say that when you're super-duper close to someone you can actually feel their pain."

"That woman's crazy," Ivy whispered. "Let's bounce, Mom."

"Good idea."

As we left the set, the last thing I heard was Jade's clueless Valley girl voice chirping, "This is, like, totally mind-bending. I don't get it . . . so Max wasn't really an assistant director?"

TALK ABOUT BAD TIMING . . . Footage of Calysta Jeffries confessing in a rehab visit has just resurfaced . . . *très embarrassant*! The timing seems especially suspicious since Sudsy prenoms are set to be announced this week. Just a coincidence? (Yeah, right!) Whether this renewed scandal will help or harm the much-snubbed Ms. Jeffries's chances remains to be seen. With *R&R*'s ex–associate producer, Randall Roberts, still under investigation and a disgruntled cast, including a bubbler who's gone to the extreme of threatening a hunger strike if she's excluded again, I'm sure the Barringers are hoping for a slew of shiny nominations to distract the WBC. Stay tuned to find out who'll take home the gold-plated statuette.

The Diva

A Cliffhanger Weekly Exclusive Interview with Legendary Showrunner Augustus Barringer Sr.

Mitch Morelli

Mr. Barringer, you're looking well. Thank you for inviting me to your extraordinary estate to conduct this interview. How are you feeling after such a long recovery?

Augustus Barringer Sr.

There's air in these tires yet, don't you doubt it. But enough about me. Don't take all day, Mitch. Shoot.

Mitch Morelli

Certainly. How do you feel about the Sudsy prenom announcements this week? *Rich and the Ruthless* and *Daring and the Damned* received eighteen nominations together. That's got to be a record. However, there's controversy regarding the Calysta Jeffries snub.

Augustus Barringer Sr.

As there should be. It's an outrage. Her performances were panoramic. Calysta Jeffries not winning a Sudsy in her estimable career is one of the great soap opera tragedies, a blemish on the industry.

Mitch Morelli

It's clear your support is solid, though her reputation is shredded in soap circles. I'm sure you've heard about the tape circulating of Calysta in rehab. I'm no conspiracy theorist but . . .

Augustus Barringer Sr.

You know this soap biz, Mitch. No secret it has flaws by the bucketful. I have the greatest admiration for Calysta, coming from nothing and making it . . . Whatever she does she does with skill and finesse.

Mitch Morelli

Any advice for Calysta?

Augustus Barringer Sr.

In my experience, when things go horribly wrong it's an indication that things could go incredibly right if you stay encouraged and circumstances play out in your favor. You come out stronger because of it. Oh, and she should sue the bums who released that footage!

Mitch Morelli

How beautiful.

Augustus Barringer Sr.

Hate fighting, especially when it upstages my show. "God wastes his time making the stars and the flowers." That's Victor Hugo.

Mitch Morelli

Mr. Barringer, who's your strongest actress?

Augustus Barringer Sr.

Calysta Jeffries.

Mitch Morelli

Strongest actor?

Augustus Barringer Sr.

Calysta Jeffries. Look, kid, you can't fake natural talent. Gender's got nothing to do with it.

Mitch Morelli

Very true. Of course, you don't have time to be on set watching actors perform, but what did you think of Calysta and Ivy's first scenes together when they aired? I understand you personally penned the lines.

Augustus Barringer Sr.

Watching mother and daughter perform together was a revelation, reminded me of why I do what I do.

Mitch Morelli

Ivy was instantly adored by daytime fans, and is arguably responsible for a boost in *R&R* ratings, not to mention getting a Sudsy prenom nod for Best Newcomer. What do you think fans are responding to?

Augustus Barringer Sr.

Simple. Like mother like daughter. The *R&R* audience sees a new generation. Ivy's full of ambition and fire. Her performances defy gravity. That little actress woke up a sleeping audience.

Mitch Morelli

So do you think with Ivy's talent and youth she can help save *R&R*?

Augustus Barringer Sr.

Sure. But not alone. In the past I seldom concerned myself with Madison Avenue mumbo-jumbo, but today's a different story. Heck, I envisaged the soaps lasting forever, and maybe *Rich and the Ruthless* won't make a liar out of me. After all, the WBC still calls my soap their chestnut, but we all know daytime drama hasn't been exempt from the financial slump. The challenge of my life is to live long enough to pull *R&R* out of the poop shoot, and I have my daughter Veronica, Calysta, Ivy, that hot shot Javier, and a few others to help me do just that.

Mitch Morelli

Does this mean we'll see more of the mother-daughter pairing on camera and you back full-time?

Augustus Barringer Sr.

Maybe. Can't show my whole hand, Mitch. Forced downtime wasn't all bad. Reflected on what I'd like to change. When the burden of this business rests on my daughter, Veronica, I expect her to excel. "It's a poor teacher whose student does not surpass him." I expect *R&R* to triple its viewership and double its sponsors! I didn't build my soaps to see them evaporate. Heck, I grew up during the Depression. We'll bounce back or my name isn't Augustus Barringer!

MEOW, MEOW, KITTENS, LOOKS LIKE THERE'S CAT-FIGHTS APLENTY ON THE SET OF THE RICH AND THE RUTHLESS. While that's nothing new, it's surprising that the sharpest claws currently belong to none other than sweet li'l Ivy Jeffries (Blue Silva). That's right, word on the set is that the fan favorite has turned into a tiny tyrant ever since her Sudsy nomination for Best Newcomer was announced. Critics agree she deftly squeezes every last drop of drama out of a scene, turning the worst writing in the world (obviously the ink of Felicia Silverstein) into dazzling performances. Ivy's wasted no time establishing herself as the bubbler to beat when it comes to front burner storylines and preferential treatment, and her efforts have not been lost on an adoring public. Looks like all that attention is creating a minimonster. In a recent *Soap Suds Digest* interview the ingénue is quoted: "I've been on *R&R* for six months and already got nominated for a Sudsy Award. What ladder?" Though looking for ways to pop her rapidly swelling head, the brass knows Ivy's responsible for *R&R* maintaining its fingernail hold on the number one Sudsy spot. So what do you get when you toss a hot, young daytime diva into the fragile balance of a soapy set full of lights, cameras, claws, and calamity? Check back to find out!

The Diva

CHAPTER 20

Desperate Daytime Diva

O ver six months, Stanley, and still no progress on getting rid of Calysta. In fact, you've doubled the problem!"

"Th-that's not fair, Edith," Stanley stammered.

"Your so-called *solution,* Ivy, called Jade a *porker.* Told her she looked like she'd packed on five pounds. Jade was hysterical and couldn't work, upending the taping schedule. Can't tell you the nightmare it was getting Wolfe to come in on his day off. Alison and Emmy refused to have their schedules altered, period. If only we could pay those bimbos based on physical depreciation. You have no idea what that delay cost production."

"But look at the ratings! Ivy's a smash hit," Stanley reminded her.

"Which is the *only* reason she's not out on her ass," Edith said, engulfed with anger. "That little bitch is out of control. I hired you to get rid of Calysta Jeffries, not bring in her mini-Calysta to add to the drama."

"It's not entirely my fault, Edith. This cast is—to put it bluntly—cuckoo for Cocoa Puffs," Stanley ranted, beginning to pace. "Emmy and Alison are constantly at each other's throats, Shannen and Javier are *in* each other's throats, and did you know Toby was almost arrested for dealing weed? Had a magician for an attorney, plus, his probation officer's a fan of *R&R* and rigged it so that if Toby got her a walk-on, Toby wouldn't do jail time. He's escorted to work with a sober coach and currently lives in a halfway house."

"So what? He's not the first."

"Edith, I need an *R&R* cast that's full-fledged, not half-baked!"

"Are you telling me you can't handle the job, Stanley?"

"Of course not," he assured her.

"*Randall* never complained like this, he did whatever it took to keep those lunatics in line," Edith said threateningly.

"But he's a criminal, he stole from the show!" Stanley protested.

"Yet every day he's looking better than you," Edith

snapped. "Let me hand you your ass, you're on probation, Stanley. I want this shit cleaned up. That means I want Calysta out, Ivy under control, and that set running like a Swiss clock, got it?"

"Yes, but—"

"And don't bother renting that tux. You won't be going to the Sudsy technical awards this year," she said dismissively.

A castrated Stanley exited Edith's office.

*   *   *

"Don't sweat the small stuff, Calysta," my tired agent, Weezi, said over the phone.

"Save your 'eye of the tiger' speech for one of your dippy young actresses, Weezi. If you think I'm over that skank Emmy releasing footage of me in rehab right before the Sudsy prenoms, you're wrong. Heifer squirreled away that friggin' video from last year to make me look bad and cheat me out of a Sudsy *again*."

"Just stay focused on the bigger picture. We'll get you your own show. As for Ivy . . ."

"What about her?" I shot.

"Put yourself first, Calysta. If your daughter doesn't shape up send her to her dad's," Weezi callously said.

"Dwayne's in Japan producing some *Housewives* knockoff and knockin' who knows what else. Ivy may be on my last nerve, but that's not an option."

"Fine, but try to let the negativity go. By the way, does

Ivy need representation?" Weezi shamelessly inquired.

"Not by you."

"C'mon, Calysta, keep it in the family."

"I shoulda known better. So this is why you finally called me back."

"I told you, I was out of the country with a new client filming in Croatia, real sensitive girl, didn't understand the director's accent, you know how it is."

"Mm-hmm."

"You're my number one, Calysta, you know that."

"I know I pay your rent. Bye, Weezi."

Even my no-account agent who I'd been with since day one was all over my daughter like white on rice. Unquestionably, the rising star on America's number one soap opera, *The Rich and the Ruthless,* was Ivy Jeffries, aka Blue Silva. And if I thought things couldn't get worse, boy was I wrong. Since the Sudsy announcements Ivy had gone from bubblicious brat to beast. But I hadn't clawed my way back, reclaiming my star on *R&R*, to see my own daughter eclipse it.

I dialed Grandma Jones. I hadn't wanted to bring her into the drama, mainly because I knew it'd hurt her to know about Ivy and me. But I needed her bedrock strength right now, her calming molasses voice.

"Y'ello?" answered a man's gravelly voice.

Confused, I questioned, "Who's this?"

"You called me. Who are you?"

"No, I called my Grandma Jones."

"Beulah? Well whaddaya know, haven't talked to you in a dog's age. Haven't changed a bit; still bossy as ya please. This is Dr. Higginbottom, darlin'. How's Hollywood treatin' ya?"

"Never mind all that. What's going on with my grandma?" I asked worriedly.

"Her high blood pressure was actin' up again but she's restin' fine now."

"Lemme talk to her," I said frantically.

"Beulah, I'd pass the phone but your grandma's sleepin'. You call back later and you'll see she's right as rain," he said reassuringly.

"Okay," I said reluctantly. "It's so hard being so far away from home, tryin' to take care of family. I miss Grandma somethin' awful," I said, trembling.

"Now, Beulah, don't you worry your pretty little head none. You know we're all family in these parts. We take care of one another."

"Yes, Doc. Thanks for watchin' over my grandma Jones. Sorry I was snippy earlier but—"

"I understand. You just take good care."

"You too, Doc." I hung up, even more concerned. I'd talked to Grandma Jones two weeks ago. Knew she didn't sound right. I'd never forgive myself if anything happened to her and I wasn't there to help. My inner compass was in overdrive and I knew something was wrong. Dead wrong.

CHAPTER 21

Be Careful What You Wish For

BLUE

I saw Dove sneaking into Barrett Fink's factory
last night. He's up to something.

RUBY

Blue, darling, you forget Dove works for Fink.

BLUE

Just thought it was weird, Dove sitting with
Vidal in his Bentley in the Lingering Shade Café
parking lot.

RUBY

I'm sure there's a perfectly good reason. Why
were you policing Dove in the first place?

BLUE

Just looking out for you . . . Mother.

RUBY

(Eyes watering)

Why, Blue, that's the first time you've ever
called me . . . Mother since we reunited.

BLUE

It's still hard to.

RUBY

I understand, my long-lost daughter.

BLUE

Not to change the subject . . . Mother . . .

RUBY

Before you say it, you're wrong about Dove. I
know him better than anyone and he's one of the
good guys.

BLUE

We'll see.

"Where's Veronica going with this moronic storyline? Bet she's just trying to fill someone's contract," a demoted Felicia Silverstein bitterly griped, reading next week's script as her office door swung open. " 'Do not disturb' was on my door. I'm in my creative process!" she said, not looking up.

"I'm afraid you'll have to put your creative process on hold."

"Veronica! I'm so sor—" Felicia sputtered.

"No worries," Veronica smoothly overrode. "I'm here to talk about a very exciting storyline."

"You mean this Dove thing?" Felicia interrupted.

"Yes," Veronica replied.

"To be honest, I don't think it's a good idea, Dove cheating on Ruby."

"I agree." Veronica smiled. "That's why it'll be Dove's identical twin brother."

"Twin brother? Dove doesn't have a twin," Felicia argued.

"He does now."

"But as it is, Ethan barely pulls off his one role as Dove, let alone . . ."

"We're on the same page, Felicia. Let me finish," Veronica insisted.

"Yes, of course."

"I've decided Ethan won't be the evil twin . . ."

"Okay," said Felicia, looking confused.

With a girly breath in her voice Veronica announced, ". . . Derrick Taylor will!"

"Derrick Taylor? What about his prime-time job?" Felicia questioned incredulously.

Ignoring the writer's sour face, Veronica continued, "It's all been sorted out. The WBC is loaning Derrick to *R&R* for two weeks during *Pathological Murders* hiatus. Isn't it exciting?" Veronica gushed, her face lighting up like a Christmas tree. "I've really missed his energy . . . I mean, the audience has."

"If you say so. Had no idea you and Derrick stayed in touch."

"We bumped into each other at a *People's Choice* after-party and hammered out an explosive storyline on napkins. Derrick's exactly the fuel *R&R* needs."

I'm sure a storyline wasn't all that got hammered, Felicia thought to herself, then: "But Ethan and Derrick look nothing alike . . ."

"When has that ever mattered in soap operas? Suspending disbelief is a prerequisite. C'mon, Felicia . . . as long as you've been in the bubble biz."

"I was just making a point."

"Yes, a very obvious one, I'm afraid," Veronica said with a dissing tone. "Anyway, Dove's long-lost twin brother comes to Whitehaven and shakes things up. Posing as Dove, the evil twin will conspire with Vidal, which, by the way, will get Wolfe off my back about not having enough camera time."

Felicia nodded, taking notes.

"Derrick and I thought it would spice things up to have his character seduce Ivy's character, *Blue* . . . leading Calysta's character, Ruby, to think her husband cheated on her with her own daughter! Incest always sells. It'll be soapaliciously scandalous."

"I'm on the edge of my seat," Felicia grunted. Taking in Veronica's dancing eyes, she added, "I've never seen you so excited before."

"Yes, well, Derrick adds so much . . . for the ratings," Veronica enthused, continuing, "Now, I'll be handling most of the writing on this storyline but I'll let you consult. Consider yourself promoted."

Felicia's forced smile looked more like one resulting from constipation. Quietly seething that she still didn't have her head writer spot back, she bit out, "Thanks, Veronica, you're too kind."

RUBY

Give it a rest, Gina, your hypno mind games
don't work on me. Dove was nowhere near you last
night, I know that for a fact.

GINA

Ruby, you're so naïve. I would've thought your
ghetto upbringing woulda made you smarter—

"Cut!" Julius said.

"What's the friggin' problem?" Emmy snapped.

"The *problem* is in my script the line is 'your *troubled* up-bringing,' not '*ghetto*.'"

"Calysta's right," Shannen added from stage right through a flimsy door.

"Are ya kiddin' me? Once again, the improv queen has a problem with me changing a word." Emmy looked to Julius for backup but he was digging his flask out of his boot.

"You know daggone right well it's not the word but what word you chose to change."

"Omigod, Calysta, not everything is some racist conspiracy. Ghetto is ghetto, it has nothing to do with being black."

I stared her down.

"Guys, Calysta's threatening me," Emmy said, backing up several steps.

"You'd love me to smack you silly again to get me fired."

"What's going on?" Stanley asked, walking onto set with Veronica and Felicia.

"Seriously, Stanley?" I asked. "You called in Veronica for this fool?"

"Called me in for what?" Veronica asked. "We came down to make an important announcement."

Behind her, the rest of the cast filed in, Alison shuffling along dead last in Jackie O sunglasses, floor-length robe, and SpongeBob SquarePants slippers. Wolfe was filming a cameo spot on another James Cameron movie while Maeve held an intern hostage as her forced audience, repeating for the zillionth time her dashed opportunity to star opposite Paul Newman in *Sweet Bird of Youth*.

"That's right, kiddos," Stanley began.

"If I may," Veronica interrupted, forcing Stanley to take a step back. "Yes, there's very exciting news. As of next week, *The Rich and the Ruthless* will be welcoming home one of its favorite sons . . . Derrick Taylor!"

Doors swung open and in strode the man himself, with swagger that wouldn't quit. Derrick gave me a wink as we peons parted like the Red Sea. Reaching Veronica, he wrapped an arm around her slender Rodarte-clad waist and smacked a kiss on her cheek, making her blush.

"Wait, what?" Ethan piped up in alarm. "Whaddaya mean Derrick's coming back? I'm Dove now!"

"Chillax, man, I'm not snakin' ya spot," Derrick drawled lazily. "B-T-W, playah, if no one's told you, step up ya shoe game—whatchu wearin', Murphy's?"

"Ethan, Derrick's coming back as Dove's evil identical twin brother, Crow," Stanley explained.

"Where'd they get *that* name from?" I said under my breath.

"I think it's awesome you're back, D," Emmy said enthusiastically. I could see the man-eater's wheels spinning.

"Thanks, sexy," he said charmingly. "I'm lookin' forward to mixin' it up with y'all again." Taking in Ivy's designer-draped model figure he added teasingly, "And some for the very first time."

Smiling ear to ear, Ivy chirped, "You're on!"

I caught that.

Beating a hasty retreat back to my dressing room, I dialed the person who was doing the most to keep me sane right now.

"Can you come over tonight?" I asked. "I really need to talk."

*   *   *

Total perfection again, my lothario whispered tender words into my neck before rolling onto his back. Only the sound of us breathing and the ocean's music lapping the beach could be heard, a faint aroma of sea salt floating in the window.

"That's my kind of conversation," he teased.

"Deeds not words." I smiled, resting my head on his glistening chest.

"Sure you don't want to get anything else off your mind?" Max asked.

"Uh-uh, we covered it. Backstabbing costars, dimming spotlight, and monster daughter," I exhaled, melting into my lover as he wrapped his strong arms around me tightly. I hadn't mentioned I was conflicted over Derrick's return; no need to discuss him with Max.

"Sorry it's been so rough for you, babe."

"Mmm. Me too. But I'm glad you're here."

After I'd discovered who Max really was, I swore I'd never give him the time of day. I let him sweat—wouldn't answer his calls, sent back flowers waiting for me at my front door, rejected dinner invitations, and, most difficult of all, passed on his hypnotizing foot rubs. But Max came after me hard, said his feelings were real, that he hadn't been using me. Though I didn't believe him initially, his persistence gained back my trust. Gotta be honest, couldn't fight the truth any longer, I was lonely. Yeah, doing the relationship thing all over again was downright scary, but I was lickin' it up like ice cream in a sugar cone.

Downstairs the front door slammed, Ivy yelling, "Whose cartoon car is in the driveway?"

Slipping on a robe, I cracked the bedroom door and watched Ivy pound up the stairs talking to herself. "Better not be Toby's. Never know what that lamer's gonna show up in."

Under sleepless stars, I shut my door, sliding back beneath the sheets into the safe caress of Max's arms.

"She's young, she'll snap out of it."

"I'm not so sure, Max."

"Like you said, backstabbing costars, dimming spotlight . . . one of those things'll make her change her tune eventually. In the meantime . . ."

THERE'S ALL KINDS OF DRAMALICIOUS LOVE MATCHES DEVELOPING ON THE RICH AND THE RUTHLESS SET . . .
And it ain't all fiction, folks. Soap suds are oozin' from office and dressing room doors everywhere. Love bubbles are brewin' to geometric proportions as FOUR daring divas have set their false eyelashes on one studly stallion with plenty of stamina. Who knew trig could be so much fun? Love in the afternoon is about to reach its kinkiest equation ever!

The Diva

CHAPTER 22

...*Because You Just Might Get It*

C'mon, my bewitching butterfly, you know you want more. One last kiss before you fly away ... before anyone suspects we're together." Derrick's enticingly smooth voice made me hot, stirring my essence. Our love boat might have sailed but I wasn't immune to the sound of that Apollo's particular brand of aural pleasure. Unfortunately, he wasn't talking to me.

I wasn't jealous, just curious. We'd had our fun in the sun eons ago; I'd moved on. My stalking days were ovah, thank goodness—all that exhausting planning and plotting.

I'd learned my lesson, vowing never to fall into those near-fatal habits again.

Whoever Derrick had in the grip of his seductive powers, girlfriend had better be on top of her game—I mean on top—and be ready to outsmart the deep, dimpled playah of the century.

"How much longer do you think we can go on like this, D, without my mother finding out about us?"

My jaw dropped. It couldn't be, I tried to reason. But it was. I'd know Ivy's voice anywhere.

"Forget her, babe. It's you who invades my thoughts all day, every day. I hunger for contact with you."

That shameless snake. And here I was playing up his much-anticipated return to the soap. Blind with rage, I pressed my ear more firmly into Derrick's dressing room door and continued to listen.

"I'm going insane with all the lies," Ivy confessed. "Mother suspects something, I can feel the tension. She'll kill us both if she ever finds out about our affair. We should end it before . . . before someone tells her."

"Won't be me."

"Oh, D, I want to spend the rest of my life with you," lilted Ivy.

"We're forever intertwined," Derrick declared. "Our secret?"

"Our secret," Ivy silkily confirmed.

"Leave all the worrying to me, babydoll. I've got your

mamacita in the palm of my hand. Always have, always will, and there ain't nothin' she can do about it."

I felt sick in the pit of my stomach. I'd just come down to see if Derrick had time to rehearse our scenes—past few days Emmy had hogged all his free time. I knew better than to eavesdrop unless prepared to hear the worst, but nothing could've prepared me for this madness.

"I was only with your mother to get closer to you. Please believe that."

"I do, D," Ivy replied.

"Sex with her was torture, knowing you were lying in the next room. You penetrated my every thought and . . ."

"Stop, D, you're repulsing me with the overshare," Ivy admonished. "Let's just talk about *our* future."

"Of course, and while we do that I'll kiss away your fears, spread your tender wings, and make sweet love to you," beckoned Derrick.

As I heaved my body back, preparing to break down the damn door and go to prison for life, a voice asked, "Calysta, what are you doing?"

It was Ben Singh, *R&R*'s production assistant, with an armful of scripts.

I knew I looked deranged, eyes bugged and bloodshot coupled with a panic-induced twitch in my right eye. I slid to the floor, a mess. Ben joined me, patting my hand.

"Calysta, you don't look so good."

Turned inside out, I covered the best way I knew how.

"Huh? Oh, I stood up too fast; was looking for the back of my earring. Just a little dizzy."

Unconvinced, Ben stared past my lie so I tried another. "Look, occasionally I get a 'private summer' . . . damn thing instantly sucks the energy right outta me."

"I see," said Ben, having no idea what I was talking about. "Right, well, Ethan's looking for you. Wants to squeeze in a rehearsal before you shoot."

"Won't help," I dryly replied.

"I'm just the messenger."

Giggles came from Derrick's room as Ben helped me to my feet.

"Thanks, Ben."

"For what?"

"For saving my life."

A completely confused Ben gathered up the scripts and walked away, shaking his head.

Never underestimate the smallest act of kindness. Ben had no idea he'd talked me down from the ledge.

I'd been brutally betrayed by my daughter and Derrick. I'd bust their asses wide open soon enough. I had to find a way to keep my cool.

"Not surprised to find you stalkin' Derrick's door, Calysta."

Whirling to face Emmy, I said, "Look who's talking—you've been all over Derrick like a wet suit since he got here."

"Jealous?"

"Girl, please, not even a dog like Derrick would bite a bone like you."

"He'd totally tap this." Emmy preened, smacking her flat butt. "Hear he packs like a python," she drooled.

Not about to tell her she was spot-on. Derrick opened the door.

"'Sup, ladies? Thought I heard voices out here."

"Hey, Derrick," Emmy flirted. "You're lookin' super fly."

"And I see you poured your fine ass into that dress," he returned.

"This ol' thing? I mean . . . thang?" she tittered, adjusting the skintight Versace knockoff.

Coming to the door from behind him, Ivy looked up and said, "Thanks for the couchin', I mean coachin', D."

"She's the reason you had your phone off the hook?" sneered Emmy.

"Our scenes are gonna be bangin'. I'm so relaxed now."

"I'd be too if I could get some face time with Derrick," Emmy said.

Giving Ivy a wink, Derrick said, "Latah, cutie."

Ivy smiled her response and slid past me stone-faced, disappearing around the corner.

"The only bangin' goin' on latah will be the sound of my gun," I threatened as I lunged at Derrick.

"Omigod, I'm calling security!" Emmy screamed.

"No need," Derrick coolly said, effortlessly taking both of my wrists into one of his hands. "Calm the hell down, I was just givin' Ivy a little coachin'."

"Is that what you call it?" I sneered, hyperventilating. "I heard ev-ev-ev-rything!"

"Calysta, we were rehearsing . . ."

"Rehearsing, my foot," I challenged. Was that possible? Sure, I hadn't actually read the whole script—we soap actors never read any scenes but our own on *The Rich and the Ruthless*. Most of us had no idea what the other storylines were and didn't care, just as long as we worked and the *R&R* check didn't bounce. But Ivy and Derrick had sounded so convincing. Was my daughter really that good?

"You never disappoint. High drama à la Calysta. How embarrassing and characteristically violent, nothing new there," Emmy said snarkily. "Derrick, can we get to our stuff? Brought you a little reward from the commissary." That nauseating heifer had a bag of his favorite chips dangling from her talons. "Salt and vinegar," she said, looking directly at me.

Stepping aside to let her in under his arm, Derrick added, "Don't trip, Calysta. Ivy and me? C'mon. Showed your ass f'nothin'."

"Look, Derrick, I've been on edge . . ."

"I ain't gonna hold it against ya this time, jus' don't make it a habit."

"Derrick, tell that demented diva to kick rocks so we can run lines," ranted Emmy.

"Fuck her," I hissed.

"Look, if you need to blow off that pent-up steam, call a brotha," he said, flirting. "Too much pressure make . . ."

"Yeah, I know."

He closed the door, an oversized gold-glittered star staring back at me. I still wasn't convinced nothing was going on between Ivy and my ex-lover.

*   *   *

"You think you can get the files I need?" Derrick recited coolly, relaxing on the black pleather dressing room couch.

Maximizing the rehearsal, Emmy leaned in, draping her body over his. "I can get you anything your heart desires."

"Uh, Emmy, you know we'll be standin' for this scene?" he asked, amused.

"Yeah, but I like to get"—she slipped one knee between his thighs—"more hands-on in rehearsal. Gets the creative juices pumpin'."

"I'm all for gettin' creative," he agreed as Emmy sucked on his earlobe. "Maybe we should keep it movin' though. I have another rehearsal after you."

Not to be deterred, Emmy recalculated. "Don't we have a love scene? Let's work on *that*."

Derrick shrugged, saying, "My favorite part of the job."

Wasting no time, Emmy straddled his lap, planting her mouth firmly on his, thrusting her tongue down his throat.

Without warning, Veronica swung in, saying, "Derr . . . what the hell?!"

Gently but firmly pushing Emmy off, Derrick wiped his mouth and stood. "Hey, V, we were . . . um, rehearsin'."

Ice-faced, Veronica said, "Really? How dedicated," hawking Emmy.

"Anything for *R&R*."

Ignoring the tramp, Veronica continued, "Derrick, I have additional scenes for you. Put your shirt on and let's discuss them."

"But we're not done rehearsing," Emmy daringly protested.

"You are now," Veronica topped, leaving Emmy freezer burned.

* * *

Partially obstructed by a potted palm, I tensely held up the menu to shadow my face as a Polo Lounge waiter snapped open my napkin. "I'll have the lobster Caesar, dressing on the side, hold the croutons and anchovies. And please take the candle away."

"Yes, madam, as you wish, but I'm afraid the anchovies are already in the dressing."

"Okay, okay."

"Will madam be dining alone?" he asked with contempt.

"Yes."

"Very well," he said with a frown, trying to take the menu.

"No, no, I'll keep it," I insisted, tightening my grip.

Hated when waiters made you feel like a loser if you were eating by yourself. Hated even more when the whole friggin' second place setting was snatched away as if in punishment.

"See if I leave a tip," I said under my breath.

Halfway across the dining area, out on the lit trellised patio, dripping with romantic bougainvillea, sat Derrick and Ivy, immersed in animated conversation. It hadn't been easy following them after they sped out in Derrick's brand-new Aston Martin.

I continued to spy over my menu. So far they'd only been talking and laughing, barely gotten through appetizers, so there was plenty of time to prove them liars. I knew it was crazy, sleuthing on my daughter and ex, but I had to be *sure* nothing was going on. You understand.

Painfully, I watched as Ivy threw her head back, their carefree laughter floating over to where I sat. Their fingers intertwined, Derrick leaned in, raising her hand to his lips while tenderly feeding her with the other. Whatever he was saying made her face melt into a dreamy gaze. I was paralyzed with jealousy.

"Omigod, it's Ruby Stargazer!" said an excited voice from a neighboring table.

"It *is* you," the fan enthused. "Told you, Herman! Calysta

Jeffries from *The Rich and the Ruthless*! I'm your *biggest* fan!"

"Shhhhh . . . I mean, thanks," I sputtered, holding the menu higher.

"You know, I boycotted the show and didn't start watchin' again till you came back. Please can I get a picture?"

Forcing a smile, I countered, "Of course, how about after dinner?"

Standing up, the fan answered happily, "I'm done eating. Herman, quick take our picture," she demanded. "A star like Ruby Stagazer doesn't have all day," forcing a camera into her husband's hands. "No, Herman, you got the thing facing us. Turn it around and press the center button. Hurry. Did you get it?"

"Yep, okay, my turn," he said.

Knowing my cover was blown, I peeked over my shoulder to find Ivy and Derrick staring disgustedly in my direction.

"Gotta admit my wife got me hooked on *R&R* after I retired. Never miss an episode."

Resigned, I took pictures with the enthusiastic fans before walking out to the terrace, loaded for bear.

"Mom? What are you doing here?"

"I could ask you both the same question. Get up, we're leaving."

"What . . ." she started.

"Calysta, thought we cleared all this up earlier." Derrick interjected.

"Herman, isn't that Derrick Taylor from *Pathological Murders* with Blue Silva from *R&R*? C'mon, let's get all three of them together. My bridge club in Rabun won't believe it."

"Don't come near my daughter ever again, Derrick!"

"You're buggin', Calysta."

"Did I or didn't I just see you all over Ivy after you told me it was nothin' more than—"

"I'm so embarrassed. Mom, were you spying on us?" Ivy angrily questioned.

"Herman, I don't think we should bother them for pictures right now. They all look so serious."

"I heard you tell Ivy, 'I was only with your mother to get closer to you.'"

"It's in the script!" Derrick exploded.

"For crissakes, Mom," Ivy added.

"Listen, I've had all the attitude I'm gonna take from you," I warned. "I heard you say 'D.'"

"As in Dove," Derrick replied.

"Excuse me, madam," the maître d' interrupted. "Is there a problem?"

"We're okay," answered Derrick.

"I'm afraid I'll have to ask you to . . ."

"We're leaving," said a mortified Ivy.

"There's nothin' shady goin' on, I ain't that low, Calysta," insisted Derrick.

"Dad would never have done this. If he weren't in Japan I'd go live with him in a heartbeat."

"Ivy," Derrick said, touching her arm, attempting to subdue the tension as diners stared.

"No, I'm not finished," she continued. "I've held this in long enough. You're jealous, Mother. Jealous of my youth and success. I'm eighteen, a woman, and just because I'm your daughter doesn't give you permission to flip out on me whenever and wherever you feel like it. I'll be in the car, *D*," she punctuated, snatching up her clutch.

The public smackdown was the last straw.

"Calysta, she didn't mean that . . ."

"Woulda slapped the living daylights outta her swollen head but didn't want to get arrested."

"She's just smellin' herself right now, she'll snap out of it," Derrick said as he left.

"Oh, she'll snap out of it, all right, even if it means I hafta snap that little neck of hers m'own damn self. She better be glad there's no expiration date on a mother's love."

CHAPTER 23

Comings and Goings

*W*hat the hell is this?" Emmy demanded, steaming into Felicia's office.

"Ever heard of knocking?"

Ignoring her, Emmy slammed a sheaf of papers on the writer's desk. "I'm practically cut out of next week's scripts! All my scenes with Derrick are now with Shannen or Calysta, which doesn't make any sense! I'm the glue for the whole Crow/Dove twin brother thingy."

"I didn't write you out, Emmy, Veronica did, so . . ."

"Veronica?"

"That's right, go crash her office," Felicia said, making a shooing motion, smarting from the intrusion.

Emmy retreated out the door, mind racing. Why the hell would Veronica do this? It felt like a punishment.

As she recalled the Derrick dressing room interruption earlier, the pieces fell into place.

* * *

Almost to her Porsche on the WBC lot, Veronica heard, "Wait up!"

Setting her jaw, she turned. "Emmy, I'm in a hurr—"

"Just wanted to tell you how amazing next week's scripts are! All that juicy stuff you've given me to do. I can always tell when you're writing for . . ."

"Didn't you get the rewrites?" Veronica interrupted.

"Rewrites? What rewrites?" Emmy asked faux cluelessly.

"I had to shave your scenes and redistribute. Actors complained you were a little top-heavy."

"Is that so?" Emmy pecked.

"The writing process is very complicated. Don't worry, you'll have plenty to do later," Veronica assured her as she slipped into her ride, leaving Emmy choking on her exhaust.

* * *

The Tranquility Tudor evening alum meeting was in full swing, with guest speaker and Shannen's ex-flame, football star Jerome McDonald, giving an emotional share.

"I lost everything. And I mean everything—wife, kid, house, boat, cars . . . you name it; even my Super Bowl ring. Couldn't find a reason to live, thought about taking myself out at the Superdome during an NFL game. A bullet to the head. But just as I reached for my piece, a kid in the stand looked up and said, 'Wow, Jerome McDonald. You're my hero!' Kid saved my life. Believe in the promises, and don't quit before the miracle happens. Thanks for letting me share."

Wish I'd heard the whole story, but the soap had run overtime again. The customary basket was passed around for a voluntary donation followed by Alcoholics Anonymous announcements, given by the meeting secretary, and our motto: "It works if you work it."

"Does anyone need a ride home tonight?" To my surprise Jerome raised his hand. I immediately offered to give him a lift. He quickly recognized me and smiled. Couldn't wait to get the full 411. Shannen would be encouraged by the news of his divorce. But on second thought, what a bummer he was exactly where he was when they first met—butt broke!

"Ahem, Calysta?"

"Omigod, Dolly B. It's been a while."

Last time I'd seen the starlet she was ninety-two pounds, strung out, and losing her hair.

"I mostly go to Hollywood meetings. But I've been sober," she said eagerly.

"That's good. Been filming?"

"In my dreams," Dolly sighed.

"So why aren't you poundin' the pavement, looking for a gig?" I asked.

"My reps dumped me and nobody else wants to take me on. Say I'm TT."

"What?" I asked.

"You know, talented but toxic."

"Oh."

"Listen, Calysta . . . do you think since I have six months clean your soap would consider hiring a young, hot movie star?"

"Hell no."

Dolly's shocked face dropped.

"Just kiddin', lighten up," I laughed.

"Oh wow, you really are a good actress," Dolly half smiled.

"I'm gonna try to talk you out of this 'cause it's totally different from anything you're used to or could imagine. Have you considered what people will say on the other side of the tracks? Soap folks without question are the step-step-step children in the entertainment industry. On top of that, there's no extra anything, Dolly. None. No craft service— not even bottled water. Hair and makeup is hair spray and lip gloss. You gotta be willing to lug your own shit to work if you want some dazzle, share dressing rooms, and deal with pompous assholes."

"No problem," Dolly confidently stated.

"Jealousy is a soap staple. Nobody'll wanna hear about your movie star career. But the most important thing of all is you gotta know your lines. *The Rich and Ruthless* is run like a GMC assembly line, and all y' get is one take and it's on to the next scene. So, you sure you still wanna be in the bubble biz?"

"Sure," she lied.

"Okay, I'll walk in your ask tomorrow to the executive producer, Veronica Barringer. She's a friend. Her dad created the show. If you're serious you should Google the soap and learn as much as you can about the backstory and the people on it."

Dolly nodded.

"Ever watched?

"Never."

"Start."

"Thanks, Calysta."

"I ain't done nothin' yet. Just don't show your ass or there'll be blood. All kinds of actors outta work lookin' for a gig, any gig. Veronica has her pick of the litter in spades, including bubblers who recently got laid off a soap web series."

"You have my word."

"I'm goin' out on a limb for you, Dolly. I'll be too through if . . ."

"Don't worry, all I want to do is work. I just need someone to give me a chance," she said sincerely.

"You mean *another* chance, don't you?" I reminded. Dolly's mug had been splattered across the rags for snagging all the wrong headlines for car crashes, arrests, and rehabs.

"Right," she acknowledged.

"Okay, lemme fish out my phone, then I gotta give Jerome a lift. Digits?"

"All I have is a burner cell," Dolly said apologetically.

"Girl, do I look like I care? Ain't nobody judging you."

"It's 310-555-4190," she whispered.

Before Dolly got up I impulsively swept her into a tight hug. Felt like I was hugging a part of myself. That determined teenager who fled Mississippi years earlier searching out her future. I felt her trembling, perhaps not wanting the affection, but I continued to hold Dolly anyway. Who loved her? Didn't know, didn't want to know. Only twenty-two, four years older than my Ivy. Couldn't imagine my daughter in this crazy circumstance. No matter what went down between us, I would always be Ivy's safety net.

I held Dolly's angelic face between my palms and examined her watery eyes. I saw a scared and vulnerable child star. My underdog spirit was stirring. How much trouble could she be?

CHAPTER 24

Drama, Drama, and Deception

*J*erome's divorced?" Shannen beamed.

"You did hear the 'no car, no house, butt broke' part, right?"

"Oh, Calysta, I don't care about that . . . much," Shannen said. "It was never about the money with Jerome. It was about the love."

"O-kay, what about Javier?"

Shannen's blue eyes widened. "Oh yeah . . . Javier. Well I didn't say I was getting back with Jerome. I'd just like to see him . . . as a friend."

"Mm-hmmm, well that's mighty friendly of you," I said.

"You won't mention it to Javier though, right?"

"Course not."

"Don't want him to get jealous over nothing," said Shannen.

"None of my business."

We were dishing in my dressing room while Production searched for Dolly Burke. She was late . . . again.

She'd been late from day one, to my extreme embarrassment, but so apologetic. She'd even admitted, "Calysta, I was so nervous my first day on *The Rich and Ruthless*, I brushed my teeth with Clearasil!" It was hard not to forgive Dolly.

Cue cards were back on set just for Dolly, making her enemy number one among the cast, with the exception of Toby, who'd taken in the starlet's fully loaded body, commenting, "That's what I call a nice chest of drawers."

Alison's wild shriek down the hall immediately changed the subject.

"What is she freakin' out about now?" I questioned.

"You haven't heard?" Shannen asked, excited to share the soap scoop.

"No." I shook my head.

"In the newest script, Dolly's character, Catalina Mariposa, is actually Vidal's illegitimate daughter!"

"*Oh* snap, they're giving Alison a grown-ass child?" I snickered.

"Yep, writers decided Vidal has a *second* family and that the real love of his life is his mistress, and Catalina is their love child."

"Veronica's the bomb. So glad she's runnin' things," I said. "Puttin' some teeth back into this patty-cake show."

"And guess who's coming on to be Vidal's mistress?" Shannen added.

"Tell me."

"Isabella Rossellini!"

"For real? Must be payin' her a grip."

"Turns out she's a longtime fan of *R&R* and was happy to do a cameo while she's here filming with Javier Bardem," Shannen finished.

"Alison's gonna go ape shit!" I exclaimed.

"Already did," Shannen confirmed. "Tried to storm Veronica's office this morning. Took Stanley and Ben to get her back downstairs. She's been locked in her dressing room ever since."

"Hate that I missed that," I said. "Wolfe'll be in heaven though. Doesn't Isabella speak, like, eight languages? I smell European lovefest."

"Calysta, Wolfe, Ivy, Jade, Dolly, Toby, five minutes, scene thirty, be camera ready," the stage manager's voice called over the intercom.

"Guess Dolly finally got here. Thanks for the update, Shannen."

"Anytime."

Whitehaven Country Club, RUBY and her
daughters, JADE and BLUE, are having dinner.
Extra diners in background — make sure they
don't speak. VIDAL and CATALINA approach RUBY's
table.

VIDAL

Ladies, allow me to introduce my daughter, Catalina Mariposa, she's been living in Switzerland.
I hope you girls can be friends.

(Get closeups of puzzled faces.)

BLUE

Howdy. I see I have more in common with Whitehaven than I thought.

VIDAL

Ruby, I don't mean to intrude, but vould you
mind? I'd like a vord vith you . . . in private.

RUBY

Of course, Vidal. By the way, I'd like to introduce my long-lost daughter, Blue Silva.

VIDAL

Vhat a beautiful creature.

RUBY

(To Jade and Blue)

Isn't she? Girls, I'll be right back.

BLUE

No problem . . . "Mother." Sure, me and my new
sis can find somethin' to talk about.

JADE

(Rolls eyes)

Doubt it.

CATALINA

(Squeezing Vidal's arm)

Aw, gee, I feel so outta place in this country
club. Do I hafta stay, Toby? I mean, Wolfe?
Awww, crap, it's Vidal, isn't it?

"Whoa-whoa-whoa-whoa, it's so confusing, all these
names to remember. But don't stop rollin'!" pleaded Dolly,
giving herself her own direction. "I'll pick it up right here. I
got it now."

CATALINA

Awww, gee . . . Dad . . . um . . .

"What's the line again?" Dolly finally asked.

"Cut!" said overqualified guest director Erroll Cockfield. The Tranquility Tudor alumnus and once legendary film director had found it difficult to regain his good standing after rehab, finding refuge in soap operas. His interim stay also gave staple director Julius a much-needed rest.

"Unbelievable!" Ivy gritted. "You have one freakin' line—on a cue card—and you still eff it up!"

"Seriously," Jade said, siding with Ivy.

"Lay off her," Toby insisted, walking onto set. "Dolly's a pro and totally badass, she's just warmin' up."

"Thanks, Toby." Dolly perked up before leveling a death glare at Jade and Ivy. "Don't worry, I don't let jealous haters get me down."

"Jealous?" Ivy scoffed. "As if."

"Ivy, stop it," I snapped at my daughter.

"Ladies, ladies, we really need to focus," interrupted Stanley Mercury. "Dolly's popularity is climbing every day. Fans can't wait to see her . . . a lot. This means good things for ratings and *The Rich and the Ruthless*."

"Thanks, Mr. Mercury," Dolly preened.

"But . . . I'm superpopular too," Ivy reminded him.

"Of course, you . . . both . . . are," Stanley said insincerely. "Plenty of storylines to go around. Now, Dolly, dear, I want you to know that I told the cameraman to pull back and make your scene a wide shot, so don't worry about the audience seeing your eyes reading the copy like Robert Wagner in that commercial."

"Okay, Stanley, but this is the first time I've ever used cue cards, I'm used to a teleprompter."

"Shhh . . . I know, Dolly, but this is daytime. Please, please try to read your lines off the one cue card correctly," he gently chided before heading back to the booth, his hand gripping his forehead.

"Next he'll say there's nothing wrong with being a front-runner for a back burner storyline," pouted Ivy. "Why does *she* get special treatment?"

"That's lunch, folks," the stage manager said.

"Damn it," Erroll exclaimed before noticing me beside him. "This is so friggin' frustrating, how does anything get done around here?"

"You're askin' me?" I said wryly, watching Ivy, Dolly, and Jade continue to bicker as they trotted off set. Toby trailed behind them, earphones plugged into his head blasting The Boxer Rebellion's "No Harm."

A hush fell over the stage as a disheveled Alison caterwauled onto set in a drunken rant.

"Abomination . . . all the goddamn blood, sweat, 'n' tears I gave to this *friggin'* show. Coulda been a star like Julia . . . that bitch, *I* was supposed to be Vivian in *Pretty Woman*," she slurred.

Wolfe stamped out his cigarette, exhaling, "Charming,"

before slipping out a side door. The rest of us stayed glued to the spectacle.

"Where's that bastard, Stanley?" an adenoidal Alison demanded.

"Right here, Alison, calm down."

"Stanley, do somethin'," she pleaded, clutching his jacket sleeves, ruched up to his elbows à la *Miami Vice*. "*I'm* Vidal's true love, not *Isabella Tortellini*! He can't have another family, I just can't—"

"What a nut job," cameraman one snarked.

"You said it, brotha. Let 'er rip, means overtime for us and Christmas is coming," laughed cameraman two.

Unclasping her hands, Stanley faux promised, "I'll see what I can do, but it's Veronica's call."

Alison careened away, bumping into Ben before pushing past Derrick, coming through the door.

"Uh, folks, how about we show Derrick some love, and let him know how much we've enjoyed having him back. Today's his last day," Stanley weakly announced.

A customary cake topped with an airbrushed image of the actor was rolled in.

"Ben, make sure Alison gets to her room safely," the stage manager whispered. "We wouldn't want folks from *Deal of the Century* seeing her, well, in this condition."

A nebbishy Ben slipped out.

Derrick gave his megawatt grin as a lowly WBC staff photographer snapped off a few photos. Nodding while holding up his palms to signal his appreciation, Derrick said, "It was real good times, people, real good times, but all good shiz must come to an end when prime time calls."

Why can't that thug at least button up his shirt? Phillip thought to himself.

"But don't worry, gang, I'll be back 'cause I'm D-Master-flow, and can't nobody replace my swagga. Cake, anyone?"

WE ALL KNOW WHAT MAKES THE WORLD GO 'ROUND, RIGHT, KIDS? Money, honey. Unfortunately, anxious execs are having to sell off their exotic car collections (I know, cry me a river, right?), while desperate suds stars consider beyond-bad soap webseries. Not-so-rich Toby Gorman is wrestling with the IRS; seems the heartthrob keeps spending more than he earns. Could jail be next? Yeah, times is tough for everyone—unless you're a Barringer. Just how much moolah they have in their coffers is anyone's guess. But I'd bet my bottom dollar it's enough to buy the penthouse of The Sherry-Netherland hotel on Fifth Ave.

The Diva

CHAPTER 25

Birds of a Feather

Randall sat in a bleak pea-soup green visiting room at Lompoc Federal Correctional Complex. His hangdog face lit up like Times Square when he saw his wife march up to the dull Plexiglas partition. Draped in rakish head-to-toe Escada, her burdened face remained hidden behind huge Jackie O's.

Randall eagerly plucked up the phone as Alison parked it and snatched hers.

"Alison, sugarplum, I've been so lonely without you," he pathetically blubbered. "It's awful in here. . . ."

"Shut up," she barked. "I didn't come to this shithole and have *skeevy security guards body-search me to listen to your crybaby bullshit."*

His balls now the size of hamster kibble, Randall zipped it.

"Every time I let you wear the pants in the family you screw it up royally. Once again it's up to me to save both our asses," Alison hissed. "I should be coasting toward luxury retirement, not the damn poorhouse. Do you realize the humiliation?"

"Oh, Alison, baby, I'm so . . ."

"Lalalalala . . . can't hear you, I'm not done. Because of your stupidity I have to start over! Pretend I want to audition for dumb commercials, and the latest—was asked if I'd be interested in starring in a skin flick. I passed."

Randall sat slump-shouldered, taking the heat.

"We've got one final shot at being king and queen of soapdom. I'm gonna get you outta this Shawshank hellhole, but you're gonna do exactly what I tell you to do or your little dick's gonna land in my grandma's meat grinder and be turned into paste."

Wincing, Randall sagged farther into his chair.

"Wrap it up, folks," the guard said.

"How long's it gonna take, Alison? I'm losing it in here."

Giving him anything but an impassioned farewell, bossyboots Alison tossed him a final insult. "I'll spring you out soon enough. Until then, grow a pair."

The sound of the diva's voice—*"your little dick's gonna land in my grandma's meat grinder and be turned into paste, your little dick's gonna land in my grandma's meat grinder and be turned into paste"*—growing louder and louder shook Randall out of his recurring nightmare. The weight of his ankle monitor reassured him he was still in one piece and not in prison . . . yet.

"They're running my character into the ground, Randy, trying to phase me out so they can get their greedy hands on my six hundred K contract and get three for one, hire more cheap labor—dumb kids like Ivy, Toby, and that druggie, Dolly Whatsherface . . . or that overrated Derrick Taylor," Alison ranted, pacing in their bedroom on the verge of a breakdown. On a dime, she went *Exorcist* on her cowering husband, "It's all your fuckin' fault!"

"Darling, I'm so sorr—"

"Oh, piss off. You better squeeze your big ass back in that executive producer seat or else."

"I promise, Alison, I'll do whatever it takes," Randall said, hyperventilating, his legs conspicuously crossed.

"Stanley does nothing but brownnose that Barringer brat, Veronica, who's deliberately destroying my legacy. I need someone who's got my hiney, and since I have no *other* options, you're gonna untuck your balls, step up to the plate, and hit a home run."

***LET ME GIVE YOU A FREE BIT OF ADVICE,
KIDDOS. . . .*** Never do in public what you don't wanna
be caught doing in private. *Cliffhanger Weekly* reports sudser fave Shannen Lassiter (Dr. Justine Lashaway, *R&R*)
was caught in an intimate clinch with washed-up footballer
Jerome McDonald. Tsk tsk, I don't think Latin hottie Javier
Vásquez will be cool with someone else's biceps wrapped
around his ladylove.

Meanwhile, Dolly Burke (Catalina Mariposa, *R&R*) was
snapped licking a "mysterious white substance" off her
fingers while partyin' it up at some club. You'd think she'd
be a bit more discreet since *The Rich and the Ruthless* has
been a defibrillator to her career. Course, the media darling's publicist released a statement insisting the substance
was "sugar substitute Splenda. It's Dolly's only vice." Ooo-
kay. And one more bit o' dish, how 'bout that scandalous
snapshot on the interwebs of *R&R* diva Calysta Jeffries
(Ruby Stargazer) draped over a hunky mystery man? Keep
checkin' in with secretsofasoapoperadiva.com for all the
scoop.

The Diva

CHAPTER 26

Extra, Extra, Read It and Weep

*I*t's not fair!" Ivy shouted, tornadoing through the kitchen. "I work my butt off, I'm effing *brilliant*, everyone *loves* me, and *R&R* gives that junky preferential treatment *and* all my lines . . . jus' 'cause people tune in to watch the 'Dolly Burke train wreck.'"

Throwing herself melodramatically onto the chair across from me, Ivy buried her head. I eyed my daughter. Torn between the knee-jerk desire to comfort her and the strong urge to gloat "I told you so," I took another sip of my morning coffee instead.

Eyes tight with anger, Ivy spluttered, "I have one scene in next week's script. One!"

I nodded. "I know, I know."

"Everyone's drooling over that stupid 'Catalina's Vidal's illegitimate daughter' crap. I mean, Dolly gets photographed with cocaine and nobody says anything. Imagine if it were me?" Ivy huffed.

I didn't want to believe Dolly had lost her sobriety but knew it was more than likely. More important, I was all ears listening to Ivy.

My little diva-in-training rolled on. "Producers reward her bad behavior . . . and I'm kicked to the curb like yesterday's news? What do I do, Mom?"

"You askin' me? Last I checked, you told me you were grown. Could handle stuff yourself," I said, flipping through a stack of mail.

Lower lip hanging out, Ivy pouted, "What's that s'posed to mean?"

Giving her an arch glance, I replied, "You're smart enough to figure it out, Ivy. I didn't raise no fool, but you've sure turned into a conceited know-it-all since you've been on *R&R*. You wanted to be in the soap biz, and now it's my turn to say, *Be careful what you wish for.* Tried to help you sidestep the land mines but you were hard-headed. What do I know? I'm just a jealous has-been, to hear you tell it. Well, don't come runnin' to me now, cryin' the blues about how

Dolly Burke stole your spotlight. You made your own bed, now you gotta lie in it. Lumps and all."

That felt so good to say. Nonchalantly, I picked up my *Soap Suds Digest*, gasping in disbelief. A picture of Max and me, leaving Nobu restaurant; the caption read: "Who's Calysta Jeffries' offscreen leading man? Turn to page 6. The answer will shock you!"

* * *

"Shit," Max said, rereading the article spilling details on who he was and how we'd met. Quotes from *R&R* cast members included: "Calysta betrayed *The Rich and the Ruthless* again. This time dallying with a rookie cop who almost destroyed the show's reputation, but then again, she's always been a few teacups short of a set." (Phillip) "I knew something was up, Calysta looked so happy. Good for her, Max is total 'man candy.' I think cops and firemen are so incredibly sexy." (Shannen) "Who cares if Calysta's dating an assistant director?" (Jade)

"The soap can't punish me over my personal life, none of their damn business any ol' way," I said. "What about you?"

Max shook his head.

Standing in front of him, bracing myself, I said, "We can always, you know, put the brakes on this until—"

"Hey," he interrupted, gently pulling me onto his lap. "No matter what happens, Calysta, this is too good to stop," he vowed before laying a kiss on my very needy lips.

* * *

At a candlelit booth tucked in an alcove at Café des Artistes, Veronica Barringer and Derrick Taylor ate oysters while Shirley Bassey sang in the background.

"To an awesome encore performance on *The Rich and the Ruthless*," Veronica toasted, holding up her glass of Le Chambertin.

"And to the sexy lady who made it happen," Derrick added, flirtatiously kissing her glass with his. "Seriously, your fine ass is killin' it as producer."

"Awww, Derrick . . ." she tittered uncharacteristically. "Must admit, I worry a lot. It's difficult managing production of both soaps, writing for *R&R*, the constant in-fighting. If it's not actors complaining about storylines, it's Dolly getting splashed across the rags, or my loser brother, Auggie, who does nothing but spend Daddy's money. And now I have to deal with this thing with Calysta. I—I don't know how much more I—"

"What thing?" Derrick interrupted with quick interest.

"Calysta's been secretly dating that cop who arrested Randall Roberts on set. He went by Max, posing as an assistant director," Veronica finished, hitting a nerve.

"She serious 'bout this guy?"

"Calysta's personal life isn't any of my business, but the show is, and the media is having a field day with the story. It's another headache to . . ."

"Everything'll die down," Derrick said, trying to comfort, though doubt lingered on his face.

"Enough about them, you were talking about me."

"Indeed I was," said Derrick, sliding closer.

"Can't tell you what it means to get some validation," Veronica said suggestively. "Don't get me wrong, I love Dad, but sometimes he forgets how hard I work and rarely acknowledges my contributions to the family business. I think he wishes I were the son he'd hoped Auggie would be," she mused, tugging on her earring.

"Well, I believe in validation . . . and lots of it," Derrick soothed. "Gotta make sure you get more R and R and less *R&R*." He winked.

Drinking in Derrick's handsome face with her wanting eyes, Veronica leaned against his chest, no longer concealing her intentions, and boldly asked, "Have any ideas?"

An hour later, the electrified pair fell through the doorway of Derrick's black and mirrored bedroom, locked in a tight embrace. Breaking their kiss, Veronica breathed, "M'horoscope *said* I'd get lucky, but I had no idea . . ."

Derrick confirmed her point with a slow grin, slipping a jacket off her naked shoulders, kissing a path down her neck.

"Oh, Derrick," Veronica gasped as his hands missed no detail of her curvaceous figure, pressing her firmly against the solid length of his ever-expanding masculinity. "Missed you."

Sliding off the rest of her threads, Veronica eagerly undid Derrick's belt.

In the perfect way to lose track of time, Derrick masterfully explored her lithe body, breasts to thighs, with his supple tongue, eliciting soft moans of paradisical pleasure from a multiclimaxing Veronica, her face conveying this was well worth the visit.

While he took full advantage of her perfumed loveliness, the image of Calysta with that detective kept annoyingly inserting itself in his mind. Derrick had a whole harem of hunnies but Calysta had always been special to him. Maybe even the one he could see goin' into playah retirement for . . . eventually. He didn't care if she hooked up with somebody, but the thought of her getting serious cooked his last grit.

Pulling Derrick's hair, then running her nails over his skull and neck, finally sinking them into his muscular back, Veronica let out a satisfied scream, "Ah, ahhh, ahhhhh!"

Angela Hagenbach's sultry song "Never Let Me Go" played in the background. Derrick knew Veronica was slinky and kinky and liked it rough. And he was ready to please.

With the power of Venus in their favor, drenched limbs melting into each other, skin tingling, the insatiable beauty wanted more. Hitting their athletic rhythm . . . again, Veronica arched her back . . . again, and in delirious excitement she half groaned, "Oh, Derrick, I'm so, so . . ."

"Tired." He hoped. But Veronica was far from "destination done." Taking direction, and after another indulgent dose of Derrick's customized *hip woo wong* with a gentle spankin', the heiress whispered, "Whew, this is a good place to rest and recover before . . ."

* * *

Cooling down, later Derrick shamelessly asked, "How serious is this thing between Calysta and the dude?"

"Why do you care?"

"Jus' askin'. She's a . . . friend. Don't wanna see her get hurt."

"Um, I'm pretty sure Calysta can handle herself," Veronica said with suspicion. "Now, how about I help you get back in bed?" she purred, slinking to the floor, crawling on all fours across the carpet.

"Gotta bounce, sexy," Derrick said, zipping up his jeans.

"Oh," a deflated Veronica replied, trying not to show her hurt, awkwardly searching for her thong.

"I ain't kickin' ya out," Derrick said with a smirk, buttoning his shirt, determined to go. "Get some beauty rest. I'll be tappin' that tail again when I get back," he added, leaving Veronica wondering what the hell had just happened.

* * *

I was peacefully wrapped in Max's arms when my doorbell rang. *Who the hell?* I thought. The chime impatiently rang again.

"I better go down," I mumbled.

"Ignore it," Max groaned.

Whoever was at my door wasn't goin' anywhere and was layin' on the bell hard.

"Shit, I'll go," said Max, reaching for his gun under the bed, which I found dangerously sexy.

"No, stay, probably Ivy . . . forgot her keys again," I said, grabbing my robe.

"Let her sleep in the car," Max growled.

"Don't give me any ideas."

Shuffling down the stairs, I drowsily checked the peephole, disbelieving who I saw.

"What the . . ." was my greeting.

"We need to talk and I ain't goin' nowhere till we do," Derrick said.

"In case you didn't notice, it's two a.m. and you're knockin' on the wrong door," I snapped, starting to close mine.

"You really dating that Keystone Kop?"

It took me a second to answer. "That's . . . that's none of your business."

"And that must be his hooptie junkin' up the place," he concluded. "How long you been seein' this jokah?"

"I believe the lady just said it's none of your business," warned Max as he opened the door wide, stepping in front of me, taking charge. Though Derrick was no shorty, Max had a couple inches on him and took full advantage of them, looking down his nose at my former flame.

"Nobody talkin' to you, Starsky," Derrick growled. "Lucky you're a bonehead cop, Chris Meloni wannabe."

"How 'bout I step outside and show you who's the bone-head," Max suggested.

"Bring it," Derrick challenged.

I was practically choking on the testosterone, and couldn't believe Derrick was in front of my house makin' a scene. I put a restraining hand on Max's shoulder before saying, "Two grown-ass men trippin'. No one's steppin' outside. Derrick, take it someplace else."

"Calysta . . ." Derrick hesitated. "Why you settlin'? You don't belong with this nobody—it's you and me and you know it!"

"Stop, Derrick. You're jus' chasin' me 'cause I'm with somebody else and your ego can't deal. Max and me are solid and I'm happy," I bit out, stepping back with Max to shut the door.

"This ain't over, Calysta," Derrick shouted. "You're too good for that fake-ass Sherlock Holmes. I ain't goin' no-where. You'll see. MacGyver be long gone and I'll be right here to catch you when you fall. Punk-ass Perry Mason."

Vroom went Derrick's engine. I jumped a little, the sound bringing back sexier times.

"I see that guy again . . ." Max began to threaten.

"Derrick ain't serious, Max," I said, hoping *he* was. Two guys wanting me at the same time was a fabulous feeling, real ego booster. But to tell you the truth, I needed Cupid to cool it.

CHAPTER 27

Meanwhile, in Whitehaven

Things were tenser than ever at R&R when I arrived the next day. Isabella Rossellini was taping her first scenes and Alison was tickin' like a time bomb. She'd traded up from her robe and slippers and stuffed her saggy tush into a body-hugging Lanvin dress and six-inch pumps.

As predicted, Wolfe and Isabella bonded like peanut butter and jelly, blithely chatting in Italian between takes about philosophers, world politics, the Venice Biennale.

Soon as "cut!" was called on my first scene of the day with harridan Maeve, I hightailed it back to my dressing room. And, man, was I *spent*. Though I tried to pace myself, knowing it would take Maeve ten takes to get her lines right, I ended up dialin' it in, feelin' like I'd just finished a triathlon.

Needing some privacy, I instead found Javier and Shannen in front of my door.

Through girlishly long lashes he begged, "Don't go from me, Shannen," grasping her hands tightly. "I will wilt, thirsting for you like a lost bumblebee."

"Javier, c'mon," Shannen said.

"I suck your lips in my dreams, *mi palomita*," he continued.

"Please stop, I'm not leaving you," Shannen assured him.

"My heart explodes in a million pieces when I think of you with another man," Javier lamented, clapping one palm against his bare chest for emphasis.

Pressing her cleavage against her paramour, Shannen said, "Javier, baby, I'm totally hot for you and no one else," falling into his arms and giving him an epic French kiss.

"Hate to break this up, guys," I interrupted, "but I gotta get into my dressing room."

"Oh, hi," Shannen said, extricating herself from Javier. "Came to check on you . . . you know, since you and Max were outed."

"Yeah, Caleesta, I heard about that too," chimed in Javier.

"Can't believe you kept it on the down low all this time, even from me," Shannen teased.

"Yeah, well . . ." I said uneasily. "Look, I gotta get ready for my next scene. Rain check?"

"Sure thing," Shannen piped before linking arms with Javier, leading him toward her own room.

I pulled my door shut, peace at last . . . at least for now.

                              VIDAL

My darling Rory, it vas so very, very hard and

veighed heavily on me to have kept this secret

from . . .

                              RORY

                            (Flinty)

Oh, somethin' was hard all right. Yeah, so what

I'm unfruitful and barren, but it's not my fault

I was born with polycystic ovary syndrome, okay?

You've humiliated me for the last time, Vidal!

How dare you prance your bastard spawn, Cata-

lina, around Whitehaven society? A child out

of wedlock with this . . . this . . . stuck-up

whore, troll bitch from hell!

"Cut!" Erroll bellowed. "Alison, that's not remotely the line."

"Rory is suffering a monumental betrayal and that's what she would say," a fired-up Alison defended, hands on hips, secretly channeling her own marriage drama for the scene.

"I have no problem with eet," Isabella kindly said. "It's good. You're sooo passionate, so dedicated. I love how you embody your character."

Furiously ignoring her, Alison scowled, "So what are we waiting for?"

"Movin on! Pick it up with Isabella's next line," Erroll fumed.

"Wait! Makeup, I need tears. I'm dry," Alison demanded.

"Visine's in the potted plant," a small voice called out, fearing for its life.

"Five, four, three, two, go!" called the stage manager.

                    ANTOINETTE

    How dare you, Rory! I will not stand for—

                      RORY

    Hold your horses, honey, I'm the one gettin' the

    shaft! I gave everything to this sh-sham of a

    marriage, you shameless interloping slut!

"Cut!" screamed Erroll, but Alison kept on going.

RORY

```
I know your type, nothin' but a lint-pickin',
tuna-eatin', beer-drinkin' bad habit—and now
that you've had a taste of lobster and champagne
you think you can sweep in and . . .
```

"What the hell is Alison doing? These aren't the lines," cried Erroll.

"You care too much, Mr. Cockfield," said Ben, dropping off a fifth of bourbon.

VIDAL

```
Rory, that's enough! Antoinette is
innocent . . .
```

CATALINA

(Entering room)

```
What's going on? I heard shouting and . . .
and . . .
```

Seeing Dolly was struggling with her lines, Isabella gently assisted, ad-libbing.

ANTOINETTE

. . . and it frightened you, didn't it, my

dear?

CATALINA

Yes! It frightened me.

(Pointing at Rory)

What's she doing here?

RORY

You keep your mouth shut, bastard child!

"Huh?" Dolly asked, confused. "Wow, that's totally not in my script."

"Cut!" an overraw Erroll shouted. "Take five, I need a cigarette."

"For crissakes, Dolly," Alison spat. "If you weren't so busy doin' the wrong kind of lines you might be able to keep up."

"Don't vhip the girl. You *vere vildly improvising* throughout d'scene. No vay I vould be able to find my own cue vith all the vierd vords you vere adding," Wolfe shot, defending Dolly.

"Excuse me?" Alison threatened.

"I understand how a seasoned actress like you can become so frustrated, but your talent can be intimidating, Rory," Isabella tried to soothe.

"It's Alison!" the diva bit out.

"Of course, Alison, please forgive me." Isabella smiled. "Eet's just . . . you're so convincingly rageful . . . sooo, how do you say-y-y, unrefined . . . so real in your role, I forget you're acting."

Flames replaced Alison's pupils after the complidis.

"Try to be patient with this young, talented actress. She'll gain understanding of spontaneity and your gift of adleebbing with more experience," Isabella added before turning to Dolly. "You're doing so well."

"Thanks, Ms. Rossellini," Dolly said, a bit smugly.

Seething, Alison didn't try to trump or backpedal, leaving the pair in brittle silence.

"Erroll's not back, guys, gotta force a break," the stage manager called. "Back in thirty. Oh, and Dolly?"

"Yes," she answered, stopping in her tracks.

"The director wants you to work on your lines before you come back to set."

"That's exactly what I plan to do."

Wolfe quickly swept in with an invitation for his new leading lady. "Isabella, please join me for lunch in my room."

"Oh, how lovely, Wolfe," she said, beaming. "Let me run to the biffy and meet you in ten."

Granite-faced, Alison snatched up her makeup kit, wondering what the hell a *biffy* was.

* * *

"Wolfe, Isabella, Alison, Dolly, Calysta, Ivy, on set for scene twelve."

Arriving on the Vinn Hansen living room set, Ivy gave me a mutinous glare before beelining it to the other side. I cut my eyes, hit my mark, and waited for the other bubblers to file in.

Wolfe and Isabella looked radiant, trading admiring glances as they glided arm in arm. A sour Alison followed behind like a caboose.

"*Vous êtes trés beau*, Wolfe," Isabella said affectionately.

"*Merci beaucoup*, mademoiselle," Wolfe returned. "*Et vous êtes trés belle.*"

"So rude," Alison hissed loudly. "We're in America. Speak English."

"My dear, did you say something?" Isabella asked innocently.

"No," Alison snapped. "Wolfe, if you're done with the Rosetta Stone bit, I'd like to discuss this scene with you."

Before turning, Wolfe said, "*Pardonnez-moi, s'il vous plaît.*"

"*Mais oui,*" Isabella replied.

"You speak French so beautifully," a much more relaxed Erroll said admiringly, stepping forward to kiss her hand.

"*Merci, Monsieur Cockfield. Parlez vous français?*" she asked.

"*Un peu, je regrette,*" he answered.

"*Quelle dommage.* But, oh, eet is so wonderful to be here, I'm having so much fun," Isabella said. "Filming is much easier than taping thees soap. I can't believe how many lines z'actors must know every day! Eet is so demanding. I could never do *theese* all the time."

"You are performing impeccably, my darling," said Erroll.

"I must tell you a little secret. When I have night shoots on a film, I sleep late the next day, order room service, and watch my guilty pleasure, *The Reech and the Ruthless*," Isabella continued. "Without volume."

"Really? Why?" asked Erroll.

"Eet is incredibly relaxing. For months I don't watch, but I can catch up in one episode. Isn't eet funny?"

"Yeah, a real barrel of laughs," said Alison, hawking Isabella from a corner.

"Isabella, to have someone of your caliber grace our small stage is a true honor."

"Gag me," cawed Alison.

"Tell me, how is filming going?" Erroll asked.

"Magneefeecent." She smiled. "And I hope to work with you on the big screen . . . once again."

"You're too kind, Isabella," Erroll said sadly.

"Are we gonna tape or what?" Alison butted in, the pervasive scent of alcohol on her breath.

"Dolly's MIA," the stage manager alerted.

"I've called her on her cell several times," said Ben. "Already checked her dressing room too—she's not there."

"What about Toby's room?" Ivy sneered. "They were all over each other earlier, it was gross."

"I'll check," Ben said, darting out.

"I hope the dear child is okay," Isabella said, concerned.

"Girl's a mess," Alison said snidely.

"The folly of youth," Isabella sighed. "Children are so enchanting . . . they keep you young."

Alison stared at her like she'd lost her mind.

"Uhhh, Erroll," Ben panted, running back on set. "Dolly's kind of . . . . I think we need to do another scene."

"Why? Is Dolly with Toby?" Erroll questioned.

"Yes, she's in his room," Ben confirmed. "But she's, um . . . incapacitated?"

"Unbelievable," I breathed. Disappointed, I darted toward Toby's room with the others. Had to see for myself. I'd put my reputation on the line for her.

At Toby's door, we were all overwhelmed by the noxious odor of food, pot, and dirty socks. Pinching my nose, I poked my head in.

Toby's walls were plastered with posters of Lady Gaga, Nicki Minaj, and Carrie Underwood. The only male source of inspiration was Gnarls Barkley. A dartboard on the back of his dressing room door had Edith Norman's face glued to it.

Every surface of the room was littered with rolling papers and commissary trays with half-eaten meals. There were empty beer bottles under the couch, where Dolly lay passed out, buck naked. Justin Timberlake's *FutureSex/Love-Sounds* blasted in the background.

Toby was under the coffee table, which was riddled with cigarette burns and covered with smears of white powder, clad in an Obama YES WE CAN T-shirt and nothing else. A small snore bubble popped out of his mouth as he cracked open one eye and slurred, "Heyyy, people, 'alk about a brew buzz."

CHAPTER 28

Afternoon with Joy

I've never been better, Joy." Dressed in a hot Temperley London, I cheesed into the talk show camera.

"Lately every time I turn on the soap you're kissin' or cussin' somebody out," the host joked.

"The *R&R* writing team's been giving me fabulous material. Not to mention the blessing of working with my real-life daughter, Ivy."

"Yes, we were hoping to have both of you on the show today. But we're delighted you could join us at least."

"Thank you, Joy."

"You must be so proud of your superstar daughter and how she's taken daytime by storm."

"Couldn't be prouder."

"The apple didn't fall far from the tree as far as her talent and beauty are concerned."

"If you say so." I smiled.

"And by the look of the prenominations . . . and I just want to say publicly I can't believe you were snubbed again. . . ."

"There's always next year, Joy. You gotta believe tomorrow'll bring a brighter day."

Did I just say that? Truth be told, I was pissed as all get-out about the snub. But definitely couldn't say how I *really* felt about the crooked voting on national television.

"By the look of this season's nominees, Ivy's a shoo-in for a Sudsy Award."

"Time will tell," I added.

"I'll be looking for you both on the red carpet and so will your fans."

"Can't wait," I pushed out. "And before I go, Joy, Ivy and I were really looking forward to sitting on this couch to-gether, as mother and daughter, but at the last minute Ivy came down with something. She wanted me to tell all of our fans how sorry she is," I fabricated.

Truthfully, Ivy and I had had another huge blowout the night before, this time over her not picking up her mess in the house and running the streets. When I told her, "You'll straighten up or else," she'd elected to leave. It wasn't the first time she'd melodramatically stormed off. She'd be back. But right now it was all about me and I had to act as if everything was smooth as glass.

Cameras don't lie. *Afternoon with Joy* was the most popular daytime talk show on the air and it happened to be owned by the WBC network. By a stroke of luck, Weezi had sold a producer on the idea that Ivy and I would make great guests for their "Mothers and Daughters in Showbiz" series. *R&R* publicist Daniel Needleman was still scratching his head, and taking plenty of heat from jealous costars who'd been trying to get on *Afternoon with Joy* for forever.

"I'm sure all of your fans out there are joining me in sending Ivy our biggest get-well wishes," Joy said with a plastic smile. "I have one last thing I want to share with you and my adoring audience."

"Oooo, I love surprises," I said.

"Good, because it took an heroic effort but my award-winning team pulled it off. Let's take a look."

A screen magically lowered as the studio lights dimmed.

Omigod, it really *was* an unexpected surprise: a montage of some of the best scenes Ivy and I had taped together on *The Rich and the Ruthless* set to Ray Charles's rendition of "You Are So Beautiful."

I welled up inside. God, I loved her. She was enormously gifted. But I knew she was treading down the wrong path, and like any mother, I wanted to protect her from mistakes

I'd made and spare her avoidable disappointments. What if it had been Ivy sprawled out naked in Toby's dressing room instead of Dolly? The thought sent chills down my spine.

Oh, no, not now. I felt a tear balancing and as much as I tried to will it from spilling it defied me. I wiped it away and in an instant the stage lights flashed on. Applause.

"Well, ladies and gentlemen, that's all the time we have with our guest today, Calysta Jeffries, better known as Ruby Stargazer on America's favorite WBC soap opera, *The Rich and the Ruthless*. Join me tomorrow for celebrity dog whisperer Sid Lamont.

"Until then, make it a good one." Joy signed off with her signature style, blowing a kiss into the camera.

"I can't thank you enough, Joy."

"Oh, honey, don't mention it. I should be thanking you. You're such a good sport."

"Oh?" I played along.

"The idea . . . my coproducers saying if Ivy wasn't doing the show to kill the segment. But God bless your agent, Weezi. As I'm sure you know, he guaranteed me you'd more than make up for Ivy's absence and you didn't disappoint. Besides, I told the producers to go fly a kite . . . that you were my generation and just as entertaining as any hot starlet."

"It was nothing," I said, trying to breathe.

"Thanks for being so gracious and professional, Calysta—not one ounce of upset on your face. You're a real pro. We'll do it again sometime. Let's get this picture for our wall and then I have to get ready to tape my next segment."

Flash went the camera, Joy was gone, and the wind was out of my sails.

"Excuse me, Ms. Stargazer, here's your gift bag and flowers," said a staffer. "We put Ivy's in the limo already."

"Why thank you."

"Ma'am, your agent, Mr. Abramowitz . . ."

"Outta the way, kid." Weezi butted in with my coat and purse in hand. "Calysta, you were outta this world. Totally controlled the conversation; they want you back. But we gotta talk," he said, pulling me out the door.

"Slow down, Weezi. What is it?"

"Your grandmother."

"What about her?"

"A Dr. Higginbottom called."

"What?" I cried.

"All he would say was that you'd better get to Greenwood fast."

"Oh God."

"I texted Ivy, she'll meet you at the airport."

"Thanks, Weezi."

"Had *R&R* move your scenes to next week. You'll have to pay for the rescheduling, those cheap bastards . . . no compassion. You're on the next plane to Greenwood. Call me when you land."

CAN'T PREP FOR A STORM Y'DON'T KNOW IS COMIN'. So let me be the first to tell ya, a sudsy blizzard's headed to Whitehaven. According to set spies, the WBC network isn't happy with weak *Rich and the Ruthless* ratings. Despite the upsurge thanks to a guest appearance from hottie Derrick Taylor and youngbloods Ivy Jeffries and Dolly Burke, ratings were far lower than expected. I hear the WBC will be employing the stratagem "If you can't make more money, spend less." I'm guessing there'll be a lot more boom shots and extras knitting in the background. As for the future of our favorite soap stars? All I can say is . . . holy contract negotiations!

The Diva

CHAPTER 29

Desperate Daytime Drama

*F*ire her," Veronica said stonily to Edith. "The same for Toby. And you too," she fumed, turning to Stanley.

"But . . . but . . . hiring Dolly wasn't my decision," he reminded her. "Fire Calysta! Wasn't she the one who suggested . . ."

"It's not Calysta's responsibility to keep the soap running smoothly, making sure embarrassments like this don't happen, Stanley, it's yours," Veronica said with scorn. "Dolly was supposedly sober," she added. A touch of bitterness crept into the heiress's voice, having nothing to do with the Dolly debacle and everything to do with Derrick's diss. He hadn't called her since their hookup. And she believed Calysta played a big part in it.

"If I may," Edith said, "firing Dolly would be premature . . . Toby too."

"And me?" Stanley added hopefully.

"I understand how mortifying the incident was for you," Edith continued, ignoring him. "Especially when it took place in front of an actress as estimable as Isabella Rossellini, but I'm sure it was just a . . . random calamity. What's important is the young actors are keeping *R&R*'s ratings at number one. Dolly's bringing a titanic amount of press to the show, and we can't afford to lose any of it."

"Meaning?" Veronica challenged.

"Meaning the WBC network can no longer justify keeping the Barringer soaps running as they are; major changes need to be made."

"I think my father should be brought in for this discussion," Veronica finally said.

"I think so too," Edith agreed with insincere sympathy. "And quickly."

"The Barringer/WBC licensing agreement still has six months before it expires and we renegotiate," Veronica reminded her.

"And the WBC Legal Department found a technicality . . . a loophole," Edith shot back.

*   *   *

As Edith's office door closed, Stanley turned to plead, "So . . . I'm not fired, right?"

"We'll see." Edith cut to the chase, pressing her fingertips into a steeple at her chin. "Veronica's disappointed with your performance, we both are. Soggy results, Stanley. I can't think of one thing you've actually done to improve *R&R*, yet you've had no problem soaking in the bubbles."

"But what about Ivy . . ."

"Oh yes, you brought in a minidiva—the show really needed another one of those," Edith spat. "Whatever happened to your grand plan? You know, the one where you were going to get rid of Calysta, who's still pestering me about *diversity* on the soap. Jeesh. It's rumored she's enlisted some civil rights group. Who needs this headache? She should be grateful she's got a job and keep her big black mouth shut."

"I agree!" Stanley said.

"You had a reputation for eliminating troublemakers that you clearly have not lived up to, Stanley."

"There's only so much I can do with Veronica around; she likes Calysta and . . ."

"Excuses, excuses," Edith said dismissively, massaging her temples. "Your future with *R&R* will be discussed at my meeting with the Barringers. Now go. I feel a migraine coming on."

*   *   *

"Never thought you'd have the guts to come talk to me face-to-face," Augustus Barringer pensively remarked as he poured a glass of Scotch from the bar in his richly furnished library, stuffed with rare and expensive books. "Must say, your courage is downright impressive."

Hesitating at first, knowing she'd get one shot at this, Alison—wrapped in a sugary pink Zuhair Murad frock—sucked it up yet again, exhaling, "From the bottom of my heart, thank you for seeing us, Augustus. I hoped I could depend on our special affection for one another."

Augustus smiled.

"Randall is eternally regretful for his stupidity," she said, head bowed in servility, Shirley Temple curls framing her face. *"Right, Randy?"*

"Right," Randall choked out with desperation, gripping the Scotch he'd been offered like a lifeline. "I may never forgive myself for betraying your trust. If only—"

" 'If only ifs and buts were candy and nuts, we'd all have a Merry Christmas,' " Augustus interrupted, sitting down in an antique scrolled leather chair. "If you believed I trusted you, you're dumber than I thought. Always knew you were the greedy, scheming type, but as long as you were doing right by my soap opera I overlooked it. This art forgery crap ambushed me. You compromised the reputation of my show, and that's what I have trouble forgiving," Augustus said, his face growing more serious.

"Please," Alison begged, going to her knees by his chair, her hands on his knee. "Randall abused the glorious opportunity you gave him, and maybe so did I, but we've seen how quickly it can all be taken away and we're humbled." Tears studded Alison's eyes as she groveled, "Randy promises on his . . . um, um . . . well, he promises he will never, ever betray you or the show again. Oh, please, Augustus, if my near thirty years on the soap mean anything to you, do us this last monumental kindness." Alison dramatically slid to the Persian carpet sobbing.

"Alison, do come up from the floor," the fatherly Augustus said with tenderness.

It was quite a performance; even Randall was impressed.

CHAPTER 30

Return to Money Road

*I*vy and I didn't speak the whole flight to Green-
ville, Mississippi, mainly because she had changed
her economy seat to first class. She'd paid for the upgrade
herself.

I leaned out of my micro-reclined coach seat to watch
the back of her head through the crack of that obnoxious
synthetic curtain flight attendants pull with a smidgen of
condescension, just enough to let the back of the bird know
"You ain't welcome up here." I'd tried to upgrade too but
apparently my spoiled daughter got the last first-class seat.

"Ruby Stargazer . . . forgive me, I don't know your real name, but I just knew it was you the second you stepped on the plane, even though you're trying to hide under that fabulous hat. Why on earth are you way back here sittin' in coach?" the impeccably groomed male flight attendant asked as his slender wrist flung two minibags of peanuts on my tiny tray table.

"Oh, I gave my seat to my daughter. It's no biggie, I fly first all the time."

"Well, I must say, you're better than me, diva, 'cause family or no family, I'd nevah give up my first class seat for nobody. . . . Anything to drink?"

"Um, yes, coffee, splash of cream. Thanks."

"Oops, it's a little bumpy today but there you go, Ruby," he said as he set down the cup, proceeding to kneel beside me. "They have me flying all over the place now, never get to watch *Rich and the Ruthless* like I used to with my honey, Clovis. But he told me Derrick Taylor was back! Omigod, all our friends got together and had a 'catch-up-on-Derrick-Taylor/Dove-Jordan' soiree. Honey, it was on and poppin'. You *do* know he's big in the community?"

"Ahem, excuse me, shouldn't you be moving the cart along?" asked an irritated passenger sitting beside me. "My wife is a nervous flyer and she'd like a gin and tonic."

"Yes, sir, I'll take care of her right away," answered the unruffled attendant. "It's been great talking with you, Ruby. Do you think I could get a picture with you to show my husband and all the guys? We just love you, diva."

"Sure, but who's gonna take it?"

Leaning in next to me, he reached back arm's length and pointed the camera phone, stood up, and rolled on.

Meeting up at baggage claim, I discovered Ivy had packed a small bag for me.

"Thank you, honey."

"No problem."

"How was your flight?" I asked, trying to open up conversation further.

"Out like a light the whole time."

"You know you missed *Afternoon with Joy* this morning?"

"Mom, don't start. How can you be thinking of a dumb talk show when Grandma's sick?"

Though I didn't 'preciate the tone, Ivy was right.

"Well, if it ain't the two prettiest ladies in all of Mississippi."

"Oh, Jacob, it's so good to see you, you have no idea."

"Who you tellin'?" he said, finishing off a MoonPie, diving in for a hug.

"Ivy, you've heard me talkin' about Jacob before."

She looked over her Prada sunglasses and curled her lips.

"Lookin' just like her mamma too," Jacob chuckled. "Can I give you two a ride?"

"Sure could use a lift to my Grandma Jones's, Jacob."

"Be my pleasure. Where's your suitcases?"

"I have the bags," Ivy said sourly. "But weren't we renting a car, Mom?"

"Not anymore," I said with a little steel.

"This all you movie stars travelin' with? Ooo-wee, thought y'all woulda had yourselves a mountain o' luggage."

"We're only here for a couple of days," Ivy said with condescension.

I coulda brained her but kept my cool.

"Right this way," Jacob said, scooping up our bags.

Ivy ripped off her shades when we stopped at the car, saying, "I'm not getting in *that*. It's a hearse!"

"Well, little miss, as a matter of fact, I use this here vehicle for more than funerals. It won't do you no harm to sit in it. Real lucky to have this car. Things been real tight since I last seen you, Calysta. Real tight. Pride-All Taxi done gone outta business and the owner gave me one of his cars as payment."

"Sorry to hear that, Jacob."

"S'all right. Silver linin' is I'm in business f'myself now. Know what they say, oatmeal's better than no meal. Been meanin' to get the air conditioning fixed," Jacob stated, courteously standing with the door open for Ivy, who was still pouting.

"Get in, Ivy!" I said. I was at the end of my rope and that wasn't a good thing.

She plopped down in the stiflingly hot crushed-velvet seat like a rag doll, bottom lip hittin' the floor, arms folded.

"It's so muggy. I'm sweating. It's disgusting."

"You'll live," I shot back.

She insolently looked out the window in silence for the entire ride to Money Road.

"Slow down, Jacob," I gently suggested.

"Beulah, just sit back and relax. Tryin' to get you to your Grandma Jones quick, safe, and on the double. Everyone's been lookin' after her real good, want you to know. Miss Whilemina and Miss Odile been makin' sure she eatin' right. Matter of fact, they at the house now."

"They know we're coming?"

"Now, Beulah, what kinda question is that? You know how fast news travels in Greenwood. Miss Bessie's nephew works at the airport. Soon as he heard y'all was on the plane, whole town knew and I hightailed it out there to get ya."

"Great," said Ivy sarcastically under her breath.

"Jacob, I'm so worried about my grandma."

"Everything's gonna work out just the way the good Lord planned it to. He in control."

And with that we pulled onto my bumpy, red-dirt road. Nostalgia immediately washed over me. It was like yesterday: Grandma Jones, Ivy, and me at the kitchen table, seventeen birthday candles flickering golden light in Ivy's full-of-life face while she made a wish, a wish that more than came true . . . and had become my nightmare.

"Omigod, Mom, roll up your window. The dust is choking me already," Ivy said, agitated, stabbing the button with her index. "What's wrong with this window?"

"Needs fixin' too," Jacob apologized.

"Figures," Ivy said snarkily.

"Not to worry, we're fine," I said, giving her a sharp-eyed MBMS, a "mad black mamma stare."

"Well, here we are, ladies," Jacob announced as he rolled to a stop next to the old persimmon tree in front of Grandma Jones's house. "I got the bags. Y'all just get inside."

"How much, Jacob?"

"Not a penny, Beulah. Just wanna help out . . . things bein' the way they are with Ms. Jones 'n'all."

"Please take it, Jacob, and don't argue," I said, slipping him a fifty.

" 'preciate it." He nodded.

Peeking out the window with an alert eye, Whilemina exclaimed, "Car!"

"Who is it?" asked Miss Odile.

"Jacob 'n' company," answered Miss Whilemina. "C'mon over here 'n' see if you can make 'em out."

"Me? Now you know I can't see diddly with these cataracts. Who's it look like?"

"Think it might be Beulah and Little Bits."

"Well go on out 'n' see f'sure. 'Cause if it ain't them we sure ain't lettin' nobody else in this here God-fearing house with Candelaria restin'."

By the time Ivy and I had crested the front porch with Jacob, Miss Whilemina was through the screen door.

"I'll be doggone. Yep, it's Beulah, and Ivy too!" she yelled through the screen enthusiastically, then swept us both up into a deep bosom hug. That was the closest I'd been to Ivy for weeks, it seemed.

"Goodness gracious, Ivy, you grownin' like a weed. Almost as tall as your mamma now, and as pretty too," Miss Whilemina added.

"Thanks," Ivy said.

"Oh, Miss Whilemina, I just wish it were happier times," I said, kissing her warm cheek. "Tell me, what happened?"

"Your grandma had a stroke," she said candidly, her soft round eyes trying to hide her concern.

"A stroke?! Why didn't anyone tell me?" I cried, my eyes welling.

"Just happened, chile," said Miss Odile, joining us. "Thank the good Lord it was a mild one and Candelaria was spared. Her speech is pretty good, just can't walk yet. We thought Doc Higginbottom would've told you already."

"No, he just said Grandma Jones's blood pressure was actin' up again and to get here right away."

"Probably didn't want to upset ya over the phone. Your grandma's been real sick lately but didn't want to worry you, made us swear not to tell you, otherwise . . ." Miss Odile trailed off.

"Let's get y'all inside," Miss Whilemina suggested. "Jacob, you can leave the bags at the top of the stairs, and get y'self a slice of applesauce cake in the kitchen."

"Yes, ma'am."

"Doc Higginbottom 'posed to be here too but he got

called away to deliver Seritta's girl CiCi's second," Miss Whilemina gossiped. "C'mon, y'all, make it snappy. Don't wanna let the flies in."

The ceiling seemed closer to the floor as I entered my old house, drinking in the familiar scents. A flood of memories hit me.

"You get you some nice mustard greens later, and plenty o' that pot liquor too. Best thing for ya," Miss Whilemina said with pride.

Sighing loudly, Ivy impatiently asked, "What are we waiting for? Let's go see her."

"Her who?" asked Miss Whilemina. "I know you ain't referrin' to your grandma like that."

"She got a chip on her shoulder, Beulah?" asked Miss Odile. "'Cause if she do she best go back outside and knock it off. We don't put up with no kind o' foolishness or disrespect 'round 'ere."

Stemming my percolating anger, I gave Ivy a chance to apologize to the elders.

"Sorry. Didn't mean to offend anyone but we don't have a lot of time. We're only staying a couple of nights. I have big scenes on *The Rich and the Ruthless* and . . ."

I backhanded my daughter right in the kisser. Sure did. It was the smack heard around Greenwood; Ivy didn't know what hit her. Enough was enough and too much was foolish.

"Now, I've had all I'm gonna take from you and that fresh mouth of yours."

"Tell 'er, Beulah," encouraged Miss Whilemina.

"You right," echoed Miss Odile.

"We're here to see Grandma Jones," I continued. "How dare you disrespect Miss Odile and Miss Whilemina? I could give a good kitty about the soap right now! And didn't you just chew me out about mentioning *Afternoon with Joy*? You give any more sass and you'll be talkin' to yourself on a plane to Japan to join your father. Don't try me."

Dead silence.

"You can sulk all you want. Ain't gonna make one bit o' difference," I finished, heart racing.

"Your mother's right," Miss Odile said.

Ivy ran out, the screen door slamming behind her.

"Hmmph," sided Miss Whilemina. "Big City do it every time. Swoll her head up real big since I last seen her."

"Ooo-wee, she's a handful, real firecracker like her mamma," chuckled Miss Odile. "Follow me."

"Doc and Jacob helped us move your grandma in the spare room down here so she didn't have to climb up them steps no more. She fell down hard when she had the stroke. Bruised herself pretty bad," reported Miss Whilemina.

We made our way down the hallway to my Grandma Jones's bedroom door.

"She restin' real peaceful," said Miss Odile.

"Goes in and out. Doc Higginbottom has her on some kinda medicine nobody can pronounce," added Miss

Whilemina. "Before ya go on in, 'member she sleeps most of the day."

"'Cept when your story comes on," said Miss Odile. "Nevah misses *R&R*. We make sure your grandma's real comfortable, get lunch, and watch together like we been doin'. She's so proud of you and Ivy."

Miss Whilemina opened the door.

"Oh, Grandma," I cried, rushing to her bedside. She'd lost so much weight. Her face was sunken, hair thinned, and onyx skin ashen.

"Now, now, dear," comforted Miss Whilemina, patting my back. "Church of the Solid Rock's prayer circle been meditatin' on a full recov'ry. She got a fifty/fifty chance. As Pastor Cyrus said, 'When your load gets heavier, ask the Lord for broader shoulders.' Beulah, I know this is very hard for you but be strong."

Between sobs I whispered, "Yes, ma'am, I'll try. Love you all so. Can't tell you how grateful I am, you takin' care of Grandma."

"Chile, thank the good Lord instead," said Miss Odile. "Wouldn't have it any other way. He put us on this earth to be of service and that's what we'll continue to do for our faithful sistah Candelaria."

"Amen," chimed in Miss Whilemina. "Your grandma appreciates all the money you send to her every month to help out. It's a blessing, honey, especially now."

"We's lifelong friends," added Miss Odile.

"Yes, ma'am," I acknowledged.

"Now, we'll be in the front room if ya need anything," Miss Whilemina assured me before closing the door.

Holding my grandmother's cool hand, I felt sadness multiply. "Grandma, why didn't you tell me? God forgive me for thinking my life was so important and losing sight of my family."

It crystalized in my mind that I'd played a big part in why Ivy was acting out—and I vowed to fix it.

*   *   *

Fanning herself in the triple-digit heat, Miss Whilemina calmly rocked on the front porch, beads of sweat studding her forehead, as Ivy sauntered back to the house barefoot, rubbing her stung cheek. She'd tried to call a taxi to take her back to the airport but found she had no cell service on Money Road.

"C'mere, chile," Miss Whilemina sternly said, slowing her rocker. "You and me gon' have a li'l chat."

"I'm sorry, but I don't feel like chatting, Miss Whilemina," Ivy said, sulking.

"Don' reckon you do, but you at least gonna listen. Now sit your skinny b'hine down and don't make me ask ya twice."

Ivy plopped down listlessly on the third porch step, moodily picking at her acrylics.

Shaking her wigged head, Miss Whilemina said, "Tsk-

tsk-tsk, can' believe the change in ya after only a year, Ivy. You were the sweetest chile. Nevah thought you'd let all that Hollywoodland phooey go to yo' head."

"Nothing's gone to my head, ma'am," Ivy said with a pout. "I don't understand what the big deal is. I'm doing what I love to do, I'm supergood and just don't want to be hassled. I'm eighteen now and don't need to follow in my mother's footsteps. It's depressing."

"Oh, so now you gonna just throw your mamma under the wagon?"

"No, it's just we're complete opposites. Everyone says so. Mom's always raging about what's wrong with stuff instead of what's right. She expects me to care about what's important to her. Plus, she's constantly looking over my shoulder. It's annoying."

"I know all about it. She calls sometimes to talk. Get advice. She only lookin' out for you and cares about makin' a difference down the lane," Whilemina reminded her. "Your mamma had to deal with a lot o' mess with those folks on that show and she jus' wants to protect ya."

"Yeah, but sometimes I think she's her own worst enemy. Bottom line, her experience isn't mine. I get along with everyone and everyone loves me on the show. Well not everyone. I mean, not Alison and Phillip, but who cares about them? They're old."

"Who?" Miss Whilemina asked.

"Sorry, Rory Lovekin and Barrett Fink."

"Oh."

"It's obvious Mom doesn't want to share the spotlight. She's been the celebrity in the family my whole life. My star's rising and there's nothing she can do to stop it. Nothing," Ivy stated with cocky certainty. "I'm young, beautiful, and talented, and won't be making a soap opera my only claim to fame."

Whilemina thought, *Lord, please forgive this chile and forgive me too for wanting to slap the livin' daylights out o' her right now.*

"Too big for your britches, if ya ask me, talkin' like that 'bout yo' mamma. You gonna have to learn the hard way."

Ivy continued to pick at her nail polish.

"You all of eighteen thinkin' you know it all, sayin', 'I don't wanna be hassled.' Yo' mamma worked hard her whole life, jus' as proud of you, and wants nothin' *but* success for ya, but the right kind. She knows if success hardens your heart you don't deserve it. Lemme ask you this, all those years she was 'the celebrity,' did she make sure you had a roof over y'head? Ever lack food or lovin'?"

Ivy stubbornly ignored the question.

"Didn't think so." Whilemina nodded. "Here yo' mamma practically raised you by herself, paved the way so you could glide on to that stage without a care in the world, and all you do is act up."

Ivy uneasily shifted her weight.

"I'm tellin' ya, get right, chile, before it's too late."

Ivy's lower lip quivered, saying carefully, "Of course I

care about Mom and hate arguing with her. But just 'cause I'm successful and didn't have to struggle and things come easily to me . . ."

"Nothin' wrong wit' things comin' a little easier, it's what we all want for our chil'ren, but ya betta darn well show some respect and appreciation."

Ivy stayed silent, digging a hole in the dirt with her big toe.

"Cat gotcha tongue?" Whilemina prodded.

"I know certain people give her a hard time on the show," Ivy began, "but they're not doing that anymore. If she'd just let it go. Why does she always have to fight everyone?"

"Ooo-eee, chile, you think I was only talkin' 'bout the *stories*? I sat you down to talk about life. Family is all we got in this world at the end of the day, and don't you be forgettin' it. I could tell ya a story but I'd be oversteppin', then again I'm old and what can yo' grandmother do ta me now?"

"What are you talking about?" Ivy asked, looking up with red-rimmed eyes.

"I'm talkin' 'bout your family history. Your mamma's childhood was no piece a cake. If you think she was on her own at seventeen 'cause she wanted to be, think again. Had no choice."

"Mom's never really talked about that time," Ivy said quietly.

"Tryin' to protect ya, I 'spect," Miss Whilemina nodded. "You get your mamma to take ya out to the cemetry on True

Bible Way. Ask her to show you your grandmother Mad-
die Mae's grave site. Ask her how she died. See if she'll say
somethin' about who her daddy was and who else is buried
there. 'Bout time you knew the truth."

"O-kay, but I don't see what that has to do with me being
on the soap opera and us always fighting," Ivy asked.

"Come talk to me afterward. Maybe you'll understan'
betta'. One thing's f'sure, she needs ya now more than evah
wit' poor Miss Candy taken sick. You'd be in there right
now with your mamma if you hadn't run off."

Feeling guilty, Ivy's vision blurred with tears.

"Your mamma don't need no back talk. What she needs
is love and a firm shoulder right now, whether she knows it
or not. You go on in the house and offer it like the good girl
I know you are. Act like ya got good sense."

"Yes, ma'am."

Slowly rocking her chair, she added, "You eighteen, it's
high time you showed up for your mamma, 'cause Lord only
knows she's been there for you."

Ivy nodded as she stood up and threw her long mocha
arms around Miss Whilemina's talcum-powdered neck before stepping back into the house with a new attitude.

* * *

Head bowed in prayer over Grandma Jones, I sat on the edge
of her bed, not looking up when the door opened. But at
Ivy's caught breath I stopped praying.

She stared at Grandma Jones's frail frame.

"Oh, Mom," Ivy cried, rushing over to kneel beside me, burying her face in my lap. "I'm so sorry about everything. I've been so out of line," she sobbed.

That was putting it mildly, but now wasn't the time. I stroked her soft hair, kissing the top of her head, before we sat tandem on the handmade crazy quilt, taking in our amazing Grandma Jones. Together, we rested our hands on hers and prayed for God's mercy to see her through.

CHAPTER 31

Love in the Afternoon Will Never Be the Same

*C*ast meetings first thing in the morning were rare. Something was definitely up, and my costars were imagining one scenario after another.

Eternally clueless, Jade guessed, "Maybe they're giving us a raise."

"Keep dreamin', honey. If anything we're all bein' canned," Maeve groused.

"Wouldn't hurt the soap if some of the chaff were let go," said a pompous Phillip.

"Chaff my . . ." Maeve retorted.

"Couldn't care less if I get axed," a hungover Dolly drawled. "My popularity's surgin' and my agent's workin' on gettin' me a Tyler Perry flick or my own series."

"That's so dope," Toby said enthusiastically. "Yeah, I got some offers in the works too, kinda wouldn't mind getting fired either."

"None of us would mind that," Alison sniffed.

"Thought I saw Randall's car downstairs," Emmy interrupted. "That's not possible, right?"

Alison didn't reply.

I kept my mouth shut too, distracted with worry about Grandma Jones. Ivy stood next to me. Our trip to Mississippi had worked its special magic and served as a reminder of what's really important: family. My Ivy came back to me, shed that attitude, and it was about time.

After putting Grandma Jones back in the hospital while we were there, leaving her to return to work had been one of the hardest things I'd ever done. Simply couldn't get my last conversation with Grandma Jones out of my head.

Monitors beeped softly in the background as Grandma Jones clasped my hand with surprising strength and whispered, "Chile, I don't know how much longer I'ma hang on. Feels like the good Lord's callin' me to his kingdom and I'm ready to go. I want you to take care of some things so you and my great-grandbaby, Ivy, can rest easier. It's not much, but everything at Greenwood City Bank is yours. All my important papers are in my black pocketbook in the bottom of my bedroom closet. And as hard as I worked for it, I want you to sell the house—"

"Grandma, no . . ."

"I said sell the house. If I come outta this operation, put me in that old folk's home—what's it called?"

"Sagewood," I said tearfully. "Please, Grandma, you're gonna be fine."

"Listen, Beulah, I don't want any foolishness. Just sell the house, but keep the land—all twenty-three acres. Dirt's more precious than gold, and don't forget it."

"Yes, ma'am."

Tears coursed down my cheeks as she drifted back to sleep.

With deep regret, I'd done as I was told and put our beloved home up for sale.

Nervous chatter ramped up as Veronica and Edith walked on set, with a nattily dressed Augustus Barringer. My heart leaped; he looked stronger since I'd last seen him.

"What is this, a funeral?" Augustus boomed. "How 'bout a warmer welcome?"

As applause sounded, I blew Mr. B a kiss. He smiled warmly.

"You look amazing, Mr. Barringer," Shannen added.

"Thanks to pure stubbornness." He beamed at her.

"Augustus, if we could . . ." Edith nudged.

"I'm getting to it. Haven't seen the whole cast like this in a while." He sighed. "You all look great and are working so hard to keep *R&R* at number one, but I am here today to make a very important announcement. The writing's been on the wall for some time. We've put it off as long as we could. After speaking with Edith and the WBC network, it's clear we need to make some big changes immediately to stay on the air. I'm not going to beat around the bush. *The Rich and the Ruthless* will be cut to a half hour."

Gasps filled the stage as the cast and crew took in the information. Ivy slipped her hand into mine and I squeezed it, whispering, "We'll get through this."

Before anyone could squawk, Augustus added, "I know it's a terrible shock, but remember, we're one of the last soap operas still on the air. Be grateful you have a job. And for godsakes, Phillip, get up from the floor."

Ethan and Javier helped the melodramatic divo to his feet as he feebly said, "It's the canary in the coal mine. We're doomed."

"Calm down," Augustus continued. "Panicking will get us nowhere. As a part of shoring up the show and adding visibility, I'm appointing *Rich and the Ruthless* ambassadors from our cast. It's an exciting time, an opportunity to reboot and retool. I need you all to be warriors; you're the best in the business, so don't lose heart."

Some stared in bewilderment while others shook their heads angrily.

"There goes my face-lift and recovery at Two Bunch

Palms," Maeve scowled. "Being a soap star these days is not a rewarding profession."

"There'll be nervous days ahead as the WBC and *The Rich and the Ruthless* team review contracts. We're rooting out the awful and the overpaid. No one is exempt. If you balk, there's the door and it's been great doing business with you. Now let's pull together and show the world how daytime is done!"

"Well said, Augustus," Edith coolly inserted, initiating gratuitous applause.

"You can count on me, boss," Ethan brownnosed.

I rolled my eyes.

"Now that that's taken care of—" Edith started.

"One more thing." Augustus paused. "And I've given this a lot of thought. I'm coming out of retirement."

Everyone broke out in wild applause while Edith coolly tapped her fingers into her left palm.

"Thank you." Augustus graciously nodded. "But I won't be doing the heavy lifting alone. My lovely and capable daughter, Veronica, will be steering this ship with me."

"Thanks, Dad," Veronica acknowledged, turning to the cast. "This is a great company because of all of you. I hope you've gotten to know me better this past year. Assisting my father as co-executive producer, I'll proudly uphold the Barringer legacy. I'll have an open-door policy, so don't hesitate to approach me if you have concerns about storylines or ideas, but please, no ghosts or extraterrestrials." No one laughed.

I caught Veronica's eye and smiled, but she looked away. What was that about?

Veronica confidently added, "Unfortunately, we've had to let Stanley Mercury go, it just wasn't the right fit. *The Rich and the Ruthless* wishes him all the best in his future endeavors."

Couldn'ta happened to a more deserving person, I thought with satisfaction.

"That said, we believe in second chances . . ."

Whispering speculation commenced between the soap stars.

". . . so dad and I are reinstating someone who, despite past errors in judgment, has given the *The Rich and the Ruthless* so much."

"That's right, I'm bringing back Randall Roberts," Augustus announced.

Emmy's face blanched as Randall emerged from behind the Fink Manor set, cheesing, as though making an appearance on *Letterman*. A smug and beaming Alison breathed in intense relief. Had to hand it to the rusted bubbler, she still had some stuff tucked in her trick bag.

"Mom, isn't this bad?" Ivy whispered.

"Nah, baby, with Augustus at the wheel Randall's gonna behave, don't you worry."

"I'm so grateful to you, Augustus, and you too, Veronica . . .

to the whole Barringer family and to you all"—Randall gestured to the huddled cast and crew—"for being so forgiving."

"Who said I forgave that numbskull?" said Maeve.

"I took the show for granted and betrayed your trust, but those days are behind me. I am mad with joy to be given another chance to be a better producer."

"Oh boy, let me sit down," said Maeve.

"Time away from the soap gave me perspective," he finished.

"That's right," Augustus said. "Randall has assured me, Veronica, and the WBC network that he is serious about mending fences and pouring everything he's got into invigorating the soap."

Augustus clapped his hands crisply. "Well, I think that's enough big news for now."

"I'd like to add something," said Edith, butting in, threading her way to Augustus. "As upsetting as these changes may be, and though you work in an atmosphere that threatens cancellation, you must remain determined and soldier on."

Veronica eyed her dad, indicating he should shut Edith down.

Ramping up, Edith continued, "This is an emotional time in America—the world, for that matter—and a critical time for the number one soap opera in America, *The Rich and the Ruthless*, America's favorite pastime, taking millions of minds off their serious problems. The media's already digging our grave, saying time's not on our side, saying who needs soap operas when we've got reality television. Meanies, all of them."

Augustus contemplated interrupting but instead let Edith ramble on like a crazed Tea Party politician.

"If we all stand united, give *The Rich and the Ruthless* everything we got, really *skate our edge*, we can make this an even stronger show, a stronger network, a better America, a better *world*," she exclaimed, arms stretched upward, shooting devil horns into the air.

The cast looked on, expressionless.

"Er, thank you, Edith," Veronica said, sidestepping. "And thanks to our superlative cast for your patience during these trying times."

An undercurrent of grumbling could be heard.

The stage manager stepped into focus, flatly stating, "Before you go back to your dressing rooms, due to the new shooting schedule, the annual Whitehaven Ball has been moved up and will tape next week. So unclip your wings and polish those tiaras."

"Feel like I have emotional whiplash," Shannen muttered to Javier. "But ooh, baby, you're gonna look so hot oiled up in that toga."

"I'll get my fan club president to get a petition going!" Phillip declared. "Fans won't stand for this half-hour madness. We must fight! 'Do not go gentle into that good night . . . Rage, rage against the dying of the light.'" he imperiously quoted. "Who's with me?"

Giving Ivy's hand another squeeze, I said, "Be right back."

"Mr. B! Mr. B!" I called, running to catch up to him at the elevator. He held out his arms and I flew into them, so thankful to receive his paternal warmth once again after I thought I'd lost him forever. A hint of his signature cologne, Eau Sauvage, hung in the air.

"Mr. B, you have no idea how happy I am you're back," I said, emotion welling in my eyes.

"As am I, my dear, as am I," he repeated, smiling benignly before stepping back to hold my shoulders. "You saying that lets me know I was missed more than I could have realized." With youthful mischievousness in his wise eyes, he remarked as he stepped on the elevator, "Let's show 'em how daytime's done, Calysta."

As the doors closed, I recalled the words Augustus had shared with me in the past: "All the people and situations of your life have only the meaning you give them . . . and when you change your thinking, you change your life, sometimes in seconds."

TWINKLE, TWINKLE, LITTLE STAR, YOU'RE FALLING, FALLING, I WONDER HOW FAR. . . . That's right, kids, I've just heard through the soapvine that it's not all wands and wings over at *The Rich and the Ruthless* as the show prepares for the annual Whitehaven Winter Costume Ball. Replete with elaborate sets, melting ice sculptures, and over-the-top costumes, it's not so glossy after all, soap spies report. Cast and crew are struggling to SQUEEEZE into a half-hour production. Let's just say the fit is oh so tight. I don't want to give it all away, but word is the White-haven Ball promises to be explosive, and it ain't all fiction. Who survives the blast—translation: the actors that make it through the savage contract axing—remains to be seen. Clutch those pearls, my pets, and stock up on the bubbly. It's going to be bumpy.

The Diva

CHAPTER 32

The Whitehaven Ball

THE RICH AND THE RUTHLESS MEMO:

Actors will be sharing dressing rooms for the White-haven Ball.

Be on time.

Be camera ready.

NO pets!

Know your lines.

Regarding wardrobe, not everyone can be a Grecian god, stop asking.

Thank you,

Randall Roberts

Associate Producer

FADE IN:

Int. Vinn Hansen Ranch great room—evening

The swanky Whitehaven Ball is in full swing, the Vinn Hansen great room transformed into a winter wonderland, crystal chandeliers, elaborate floral arrangements on every white-linen-covered table, and soft billows of mist crossing the floor (keep it subtle with the fog machine). Bedazzled costumed guests fill the room, dancing and drinking, laughing and talking (make sure the extras mouth their conversations and don't eat the food) while soft music is played by the Whitehaven Chamber Orchestra (make sure extras don't play the instruments). Entire cast will be dancing on the floor. VIDAL—in Double 007 attire—approaches RUBY.

VIDAL

Ruby, so pleased you could make the Whitehaven Ball this year. You look ravishing as a Renaissance princess.

RUBY

Thanks, Vidal. Wild horses couldn't keep me from this shindig. And again, congrats on being reunited with your long-lost daughter, Catalina.

VIDAL

Thank you, Ruby. How are things with your long-lost daughter, Blue?

RUBY

Let's just say I know what you're going through.

VIDAL

And despite our personal upheavals we keep going. My Catalina's a lovely girl, it's as though I've known her all my life—

RORY

(Icily interrupting)

That brat's a pain in the—

VIDAL

Rory, please . . .

RORY

(Rolling her eyes)

Yeah, yeah . . . now's not the time, but when

is? Ruby, would you excuse us? I need to talk to
my husband . . . alone.

RUBY

No problem, gotta talk to my hubby too. He's
been a mess since his evil twin brother, Crow,
came to town.

RORY

We got our own problems. Vidal. A word?

(Vidal leaves Ruby with a nod)

*Suddenly a shadowy figure in the corner
catches Ruby's eye—it's Queenie! Barrett Fink's
longtime maid and Ruby's long-lost mother, who
has been dead for a year. Ruby steps closer and
the image vanishes among the guests. Was it a
ghost? Shaken, Ruby turns to join her newfound
daughter, Blue, and Catalina.*

RUBY

Hello . . .

BLUE

(Coldly)

Look, I don't think we have anything to say to

each other . . . ever since you accused me of sleeping with your husband.

RUBY

That's not fair, Blue! How was I supposed to know my husband had a twin named Crow? What was I to think, walking in on you with a man that's identical to my husband, right down to the birthmark on his—

CATALINA

Maybe I should give you two some space.

BLUE

That won't be necessary, Catalina. My 'mother,' Ruby, and I are done . . . forever.

RUBY

Blue, you're my daughter, and despite everything that's happened, we can't lose each other again.

CATALINA

Your mom's right, Blue. Even though I'm Vidal Vinn Hansen's love child and stuff, I wouldn't give up my relationship with my new dad for anything, no matter how straightened . . .

"Cut," Erroll called. "Dolly, dear, the word is *strained*, not *straightened*."

"Oh, wow, I thought that was a typo," she said blankly.

I watched Ivy bite her tongue, saying with forced politeness, "You were doing really well up to that point, Dolly."

I was proud of Ivy for trying.

"Thanks! I've totally been practicing."

"Are you kidding me with this crap?" an exasperated Emmy butt in from the Vinn Hansen mansion doorway where she'd been waiting in fake snow to enter. Fashionably boney, she was sparkle-farkled to death, with gold serpent bracelets winding up her pencil-thin arms. Draped in a peplos barely reaching the tops of her thighs and strapped in Roberto Cavalli sandals, she bitched, "We're on a friggin' half-hour schedule and this bimbo's getting a pat on the back for getting half her lines right? Her scene's like watching paint dry."

"Everyone, take five," said the stage manager.

High-strung Emmy was grumpier than usual since Randall had come back.

I had my own—far more important—things to deal with at home. Grandma Jones was slowly recovering and I was trying to convince her to move out to California and live with me and Ivy in Malibu. Doctors said she wasn't strong enough to travel anytime soon and she was still insisting on going into Sagewood Retirement Home in Mississippi. She said she didn't want to be a burden on anyone. The thought of it broke my heart.

Everyone took a double take as Phillip entered in a skin-tight Grecian tunic helped by men's Spanks, leaving nothing to the imagination. Lace-up sandals adorned his freshly waxed legs, with a spray of Caesar laurel crowning his head and a sprinkle of gold dust on his face and arms. On Javier, the look might have been hot; on Phillip it was a definite fail.

"Emmy, what the hell do you think you're doing?" he demanded. "I'm supposed to be the only Grecian. You're supposed to be in the Bo Peep dress, remember?"

"I passed on that costume. Wouldn't be caught dead in that Pepto pink mess," Emmy countered. "It gave me hives when I tried it on in the fitting. Besides, this is so gladiator chic, more me and what my fans expect."

"You have no idea what you're talking about," Phillip said furiously. "I worked hard designing this costume for my Barrett Fink character. Get your own look! Plus, we can see the bottoms of your butt cheeks," he grimaced.

"There's no wrong way to wear this thing. Jealous?" Emmy teased.

"Phillip, you both look fantastic," said Erroll, diplomatically intervening. "You only have one scene together, I'm sure the audience won't mind."

"Yeah, sit down, Caesar, and hit your reset button," Emmy said snidely.

"*PLACES,*" screamed the stage manager.

* * *

"What a mess," I muttered in the refuge of my dressing room, tearing off the two-hundred-pound velvet Renaissance monstrosity. It could've been worse. I'd turned down the fire-red Satan jumpsuit that Toby was now gleefully wearing, poking people with his plastic pitchfork.

A soft knock sounded and Ivy came in, looking beautiful in her Tinker Bell costume. We were sharing my room since hers was being used by guest actor Bonnie Blackburn, playing back-from-the-dead-yet-again villainess Uranus Winterberry, who was sure to cause some kind of havoc at the Whitehaven Ball, though no one knew what. It had been decided by the *R&R* brass not to give the cast the last act of the script, to avoid spoilers and leaks to the press.

"These cheap heels are killing me," Ivy said, plopping down on my couch.

"Just be glad you're not in that devil costume. Toby already has a creepy rash on his back. On second thought, I'm not so sure that's from the costume," I joked.

"Ew, mom!" Ivy laughed.

I'd hoped it would be like this from the beginning, the two of us united on this absurd set.

"What's goin' on outside?" I asked.

"*Cliffhanger Weekly*'s here, interviewing Emmy," Ivy said, adjusting her wings.

"Yeah, for the Sudsy Awards feature," I said dryly.

"Did you hear the WBC got Drew Barrymore and Woody Harrelson to host the Sudsys this year?"

"No."

"Mom, I'm so sorry. You should've been nominated, not me."

"Oh, baby, I'm so happy for you," I said. "You deserve your nomination. I couldn't be prouder. And you know what else?"

"What?" she asked.

"You're gonna win."

"Oh, Mom, do you think so?"

"I know so, pumpkin, I can just feel it."

Ivy laid her head on my shoulder.

Another knock interrupted our mother-daughter moment, and a delirious Shannen burst in. Looking drop-dead sexy dressed as a go-go dancer in white vinyl hot pants and matching thigh-high boots, her blond hair was pulled back in a tight ponytail, thick sixties makeup framing her blue eyes.

"I'm sorry, guys, but I have to talk to you," she said breathlessly.

"What is it?" I asked, motioning for her to take a seat.

Choosing to pace instead, she blurted out, "My ex, Roger, got a book deal."

"What?" I asked.

"You heard me. Roger got a goddamn book deal! *From prison*. A *six-figure tell-all* book deal," she exclaimed, distraught. "I don't know what's worse . . . that it's a tell-all or that he's getting six figures." Shannen dramatically collapsed onto the couch, holding her head in her hands.

"Look, girl, it sucks you don't get some of the payola, but I don't think you have to worry. I mean, what can he really say about you?"

Shannen raised her head to give a tragic look.

"Okay, well, if he says anything too . . . scandalous you can always sue," I suggested. "Defamation of character. Shan, nobody really remembers you guys as a couple anymore. You've done a good job distancing yourself from that jackass."

"I hope you're right, Calysta. I'm so relieved our cabin in Big Bear finally sold, been on the market for months. It was my last tie to him."

"There ya go." I nodded. "The book's gonna tank, watch. Probably won't sell one copy."

"Well, I don't care if it's gold-leafed, I don't want to be mentioned in it," Shannen said dramatically.

*　*　*

"Thanks for the interview, Emmy," Mitch Morelli said, wrapping up. "Before I go, anything to add about the hosts the WBC nabbed for the 2012 Sudsy Awards in Vegas?"

"Drew's a cutie pie and Woody's effin' hot, and I intend to . . ." The determined diva winked.

"I'm sure."

"When Woody rips open that Sudsy envelope and reads, 'And the Sudsy goes to Emmy Abernathy for Best Leading

Actress in a Daytime Drama on *The Rich and the Ruthless*,'
I'm going to slowly vamp my way up that staircase for extra
camera time, bump Drew outta the frame, and lay a hot lip-
lock on the Woodsman."

"He's married," Mitch warned.

"Yeah, isn't that great!" Emmy said, miles away in her
fantasy.

"Emmy? Emmy?" Mitch called, attempting to shake the
bubbler out of her delusion.

"Tell us about your dazzling costume—what was your
inspiration?"

"Hmm? Oh, it's a Gaga-gladiator hybrid."

"So the costume is Roman with a pop slant?"

"Yeah, sure. Now ask me about these babies"—indicating
her serpent bracelets—"they're more than just bracelets."

"How do you mean?" Mitch asked.

"Snakes are known to ward off evil spirits and there's no
shortage of those on this set," she scoffed.

"Snakes or evil spirits?"

"Both."

"Anyone you care to name?"

"Tryin' to get me fired, Mitch?"

"Fair enough," Mitch said, calculatingly. "How about a
quote about Calysta Jeffries's return to *The Rich and the Ruthless*? Reviews have been fabulous and the show's viewership
has been showing signs of an increase. Have you two been
working well together?"

Emmy twisted the right side of her lips into a tight knot, saying, "Sure. Though I have my antivenom serum just in case."

"Emmy!"

"Just kidding," she bit. "For crissakes, where's your sense of humor, Mitch? I couldn't be happier Calysta's back on the soap, with her spawn. She sure has come a long way from that horrible DUI—didja see that tape? Nothing short of transformational. She's still a little fragile so I give her as many *takes* as she needs until she gets back up on her little tootsies. Gonna ask me anything else?"

Internally rolling his eyes, Mitch pressed on. "How do you feel having Randall Roberts back on the *R&R* set?"

Emmy's face hardened into marble. "Interview's over."

✳   ✳   ✳

"For a show that's just reduced itself to a stinkin' half hour, how the hell are they affording all these ice sculptures and crystal crap?" Alison groused to Maeve at Craft Service, gnawing on a bagel thick with cream cheese.

"In four words: *Augustus Barringer is back*," Maeve asserted. "Remember when we had real champagne and oysters on the show?"

Alison nodded.

"Now they make us eat disgusting fish parts they call crab. Every time I have to eat it on camera I do my best acting."

"Maybe you should eat more of them," Alison said cattily.

Toby bounded up to them, carrying a plate piled high with the fake seafood, asking, "Want some?"

"No thanks," the divas said in unison.

"Man, I love this stuff. Sauce is smokin'."

Wrinkling her nose, Alison said, "It's ketchup."

"Bitchin'!" Oblivious, Toby continued, "Ball's a blast, woulda been better though if the show booked MF Doom."

The aging bubblettes glared wordlessly.

FADE IN:

Int. Vinn Hansen Ranch great room—late evening.

The ball is at its height of merriment. The cast are all on the floor. No one sees Uranus Winterberry in her Phantom of the Opera costume skulk downstairs to the basement.

VIDAL

(Hoarsely whispering)

Rory, enough about my darling daughter, Catalina. You've driven off her mother, Antoinette, who, I confess, I still care for, but I vill not allow you to intimidate my recently found child.

Vhether you accept it or not, she is my flesh and blood. Don't make me choose.

RORY

(Hissing)

Like mother, like daughter, both vile creatures. And a complete embarrassment to me. You should've let Catalina run down your leg.

VIDAL

That is disgusting, Rory. I'm varning you. My daughter stays in Vhitehaven and that's final.

(Vidal stalks off)

RORY

(To herself, menacingly)

We'll see about that once I collect your sperm and one of her tampons and get the results of a paternity test.

Cut to:

BLUE

(With Catalina, watching Vidal and Rory)

I honestly don't know what he sees in that dusty bimbo, Rory. Sorry, she's your stepmom.

CATALINA

Me too, Vidal's way too good for her.

BLUE

He should be with someone like me.

CATALINA

(Laughing)

You're so bad, Blue! Hey, have you thought about what I said about your mom . . . Ruby?

BLUE

Yeah, but she thought I slept with her husband, Dove.

CATALINA

Just make up with her before anything happens. Seriously, we're kinda in the same boat. I was left in some boarding school in Switzerland and you were in some pathetic group home for foster kids, right?

> *(Blue nods, fire in her eyes)*

So, get in the chips while you can. Your mom's rich. Why should that bratty half sister of yours, Jade, get all the goods?

(Reaction from Blue)

Something could totally happen and then it would
be too bad, so sad.

"I did it!" Dolly exclaimed triumphantly, jumping up and down, ecstatic she hadn't made one gaffe in delivering her extensive lines.

"The scene's not over," Ivy whispered through her teeth.

Watching the monitors in the control room with Veronica and Randall, Erroll picked up the ringing phone. "Yes, Edith, whatever you say. . . . Keep rolling," he told the crew, "we'll fix it in editing. Is everyone on the floor?" Erroll asked wearily.

"Yes," answered the stage manager into his headset.

"Okay, tell Special Effects to give it all they got, we're only doing this damn scene once. Action on the explosion. . . ."

Carefree Whitehaven society dancing the
night away are suddenly caught off guard when a
massive life-or-death explosion rocks the Vinn
Hansen Ranch. A main gas line has ruptured.
Chaos and confusion. Screams and choking dust
fill the air as the walls buckle, on the brink
of collapse. Overhead, the stained-glass ceiling

violently cracks. Ruby, Vidal, Gina, Barrett, Rory, and the entire cast look up, then attempt to scramble to safety, finding the ballroom doors locked. The priceless Tiffany ceiling perilously plummets onto the crowned and tiara'd, burying the Whitehaven guests.

(Fade to black)

Who survives is anyone's guess. But be sure and get the whole scoop in the next Secrets of a Soap Opera Diva tell-all!

Author's Note

Dear Soap Opera Devotees,

Thank you for sliding into the fictional swirl of your favorite sudser day after day, year after year. For many of you, your favorite soap opera has been shared and passed down like a prized heirloom, most likely from a mother or grandmother.

While many credit the legendary Irna Phillips as having caused the daytime soap opera to become an international phenomenon, and more notably the most lucrative form of branded content in the history of advertising, it was actually husband-and-wife writing team Frank and Anne Hummert who first realized what a profitable prospect airing the scripted pathos and passions of some very desperate housewives could be.

Many diehard soap enthusiasts unapologetically rearrange lunch breaks and reschedule doctor appointments around their "love in the afternoon" so not to miss one second of cliff-hanger suspense. Fans around the world would defend, "It's a way to put real life on hold—unplug and unwind."

The "stories" allow grown men and women to laugh one minute and cry the next. Unintentionally interactive, soaps encourage viewers to talk out loud, giving advice to their favorite characters on the television screen.

Some have reported how their beloved sudser not only kept them company but engaged them in one of their favorite pastimes—they were keeping up with extended family members on the tube. Knowing they could depend on the companionship of a soap opera made it more than a daytime drama, rather a lifeline.

For soap fans around the globe, it's been a challenging season for the soap opera industry, but one thing's for sure: there are no fans more loyal than you, continuing to tune in, unable to resist the soapalicious temptation of witnessing who will slip off the cliff next.

Your favorite daytime diva looks forward to hearing from you real soon.

Bubbles and kisses,
Victoria
Twitter: @victoriarowell
www.victoriarowell.com

Acknowledgments

I'm indebted to:

Simon & Schuster/Atria publishers, especially my impossibly chic editor, Malaika Adero, for making this another unforgettable experience.

My literary agent, Irene Webb, for your gentle support and steadfastness. Lisa and Liz at The Moore Firm in Atlanta. My brilliant manager, Keith Schoen; agent, Rebecca Shrager at People Store; and the Geddes Agency, for keeping all the balls in the air. The Hambidge Center for Creative Arts and Sciences fellowship, for providing such a poetic space to write.

The fans, for your enduring support of me as an actress and a writer.

My amazing children, Maya and Jasper, for always inspiring me and reminding me "Mom, it's not that serious."

My yoga teacher, Bethany, omigod, if it weren't for you and Red Hot Yoga . . .

And my extended family of girlfriends, I simply couldn't do it without you.